I ♥ THE EARL

Also by Caroline Linden

I THE EARL

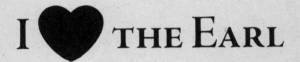

CAROLINE LINDEN

AVONIMPULSE

I LOVE THE EARL. Copyright © 2011 by P. F. Belsley. All rights reserved under International and Pan-American Copyright Conventions. By payment of the required fees, you have been granted the nonexclusive, nontransferable right to access and read the text of this e-book on-screen. No part of this text may be reproduced, transmitted, downloaded, decompiled, reverse engineered, or stored in or introduced into any information storage and retrieval system, in any form or by any means, whether electronic or mechanical, now known or hereinafter invented, without the express written permission of HarperCollins e-books.

EPub Edition August 2011 ISBN: 9780062109477

Print Edition ISBN: 9780062115751

10 9 8 7 6

CHAPTER ONE

When Margaret de Lacey was six years old, she dreamed of being a great beauty and marrying a prince. Her mother laughed and said of course she would, if only she ate her porridge and did as her nurse said. Margaret obeyed, although she wasn't sure what porridge had to do with beauty. But Mama was very beautiful, and therefore she must know the secret.

When she was ten years old, the local squire's son called her a horse-faced shrew. Her brother showed Margaret how to punch a boy right in the nose, and she felt much better after showing the squire's son this new skill, even if it did result in a fortnight's punishment for unladylike behavior.

When she was fourteen, she threw her mirror against the wall and broke it, furious at the reflection it showed her. She wanted to be dainty and beautiful, not tall and plain with no bosom to speak of. She didn't want to hear about ducklings and swans anymore, or about good bones or fine eyes. No one cared about those things any more than they cared about her talents on the pianoforte or whether she could speak French.

By the time Margaret was seventeen, she accepted, however

sullenly and grudgingly, that the best she could hope for was
to be called charming, or perhaps handsome. Her father told
her handsome was better than beautiful, for beauty faded and
handsome lasted a lifetime. Margaret smiled and laughed with
her dear papa, but privately she knew he lied. He had married
a beautiful woman who was still beautiful. And gentlemen in
London didn't seem much interested in "handsome" young
ladies in any event, not in either of Margaret's Seasons in town,
and she ended them both as she had begun: unmarried, at
home.

When she was twenty-one, she accepted that she would be
a spinster all her life. Though far from destitute, she was also
far from rich. Her father was the grandson of a duke, but due
to a falling out some years ago, they weren't at liberty to presume on that connection. And young ladies with no fortune,
tenuous connections, and little beauty were too common in
England for Margaret to stand out.

When she was twenty-five, her mother died of a cancer. For
three years she ran her father's household, until he caught a chill
in a November rainstorm and passed away before Christmas.
That left Margaret, nearing thirty, to her brother's charity.

Francis was ten years her elder, and as such he had been
either an adored god-like figure or absent, first at school and
then in London. He had also never married, and since he was
fond of living well, it was a far better situation than most spinsters suffered, even if it did require her to uproot from her
home in the country and move to London. Margaret knew all
this, but she still thought it cruel of the Fates to sentence her to
being her brother's companion for life.

"Cheer up, Meg," Francis told her over dinner the first

night she was under his roof. "I'm glad you're unmarried. Now I shan't have to hire a new housekeeper."

"I will poison your food if you ever say that to me again," Margaret replied. "Once you marry, I plan to steal a large sum of money from you and run off to Italy to have scandalous affairs."

He laughed. "A fine thing to say to the brother who took you in off the street! Besides, I shall never marry. I'm far too old and gray."

She gave him a sour look. Her brother was tall and vigorous, and looked ten years younger than he was. Many called him handsome, and unlike in Margaret's case, it was meant in a complimentary way. "You're hardly gray at all, and unlike women, men can marry whenever they want."

He scoffed. "Not true—not that I intend to marry. I prefer the bachelor life."

This was probably true. For as long as Margaret could remember, Francis had been determined to chart his own course. From the moment he reached adulthood and bolted for London, she'd heard the slightly shocked whispers about him, although due to the age gap between them, she didn't understand the stories at first. He really had been a rake and a scoundrel, but Margaret also knew him to be fiercely loyal and protective. He would make a good husband, if only he set his mind to it.

"I'll poison us both if you expect me to live with you forever," she said. "You'll marry. You'd make a good father—you would, Francis, don't scowl at me—and someday you'll want a steady companion for your old age. And I shan't be her," she added as he started to smirk.

"You're a romantic." He pointed a fork at her. "Take my word for it, marriage isn't like that rot poets and novelists portray. It's a damned cage. Some don't realize it until the door is locked tight behind them, but they're prisoners all the same."

She sighed. "Don't worry. I'm not likely to ever know the difference."

As often happens, however, fate conspired against both of them. In the spring, their distant cousin Arthur died of consumption. Margaret read the news in the paper and pointed it out to Francis, who merely grunted. Neither had ever met Arthur, due to the long-standing breach in their family, and neither paid much heed to the news of his death until a fortnight later, when a letter arrived.

It caused a bit of a stir in the household, arriving in the hand of a tall, stone-faced footman wearing the buff and green livery of the Duke of Durham. Margaret studied the crest embossed in the smear of wax sealing the missive. The duke was the late Arthur's father, and great-uncle to Margaret and Francis. Not that it had ever mattered before; they hadn't spoken to that side of the family in Margaret's lifetime. But something about this letter made her skin prickle with premonition.

When Francis returned home, he read the letter in silence. "Durham requests my presence," was all he would tell her, but Margaret was no fool. She slipped into Francis's study and read the peerage, until she realized exactly what must be on Durham's mind. Arthur's older brother Philip had died years ago, and the duke had no more sons. Margaret's grandfather had been the duke's younger brother, and her father had been his only son, who in turn had only one son—her brother. Francis was the new heir presumptive to the dukedom of Durham.

"Don't make too much of it," he warned when she confronted him about it. "Durham is a bitter old man. I wouldn't put it past him to have a new young bride within the week, trying to sire another son."

"He's ninety!"

"And he hated our grandfather," Francis said coldly. "Don't underestimate the curative powers of spite."

But Durham didn't, or couldn't, find a young bride in time. By that autumn he contracted a slow wasting disease. Late one night in the dead of winter, a tall, spare man knocked on the de Lacey town house door. "I bring news," he announced in a deep voice that carried up the stairs to where Margaret hovered, shamelessly eavesdropping, while Francis went down to see the caller. "His Grace, the Duke of Durham, has died this evening. By patent, the title and its encumbrances descend to you." A pause. "Your Grace."

Margaret never heard Francis's reply. The air seemed to have left the room. She sank to the stairs, gasping for breath. She was the sister of a duke. She could hardly comprehend it, and from the expression on his face when the solicitor left— for it was the Duke of Durham's solicitor who had brought the news—neither could her brother.

"This will change everything, Meg," he said heavily, sinking into his favorite leather chair.

"Yes—a dukedom!" She shook her head. "Wouldn't Papa have enjoyed the sight of this?"

"Not if he had any sense," muttered her brother.

Margaret knelt beside him and took his hand. "Are you worried, Francis? Because I believe you'll make a fine duke. Look how well you've done for yourself already." She swept one hand around the room, encompassing their comfortable furnishings. She knew her brother wasn't truly wealthy, but he had done quite well with his business enterprises, and certainly wasn't poor.

"Managing a dukedom is quite a different thing than playing at investments."

"Yes," she allowed. "But you're no naïve young man to be abused by sycophants and swindlers." She paused. "And I shall have my revenge on you: Now you have no choice but to marry."

A queer expression crossed his face. "No."

Margaret, who had seen the way unmarried ladies threw themselves at any man with a ducal crown, just smirked. "You'll be fortunate to escape the salons of London without a dozen eager brides chasing you."

Francis flinched. "Heaven help me."

"Don't say you're frightened at the thought of being pursued by beautiful women!"

"Like a fox with a crippled leg, set on by a pack of hungry hounds," he said grimly.

Margaret laughed, but stopped when she saw her brother's face. He was genuinely uneasy, with a trapped, almost panicked look about him. "Francis, what is it? Most people would see this as a brilliant stroke of good fortune." She glanced around the well-appointed room. Their home was gracious and comfortable, but would surely pale next to the Durham properties. Her brother was ambitious and driven, and had made his own small fortune already. If he could do this well when he had started with so little, she was sure he would own half of England, given Durham's resources. Why wasn't he pleased at the boundless opportunity just laid at his feet?

For a long time he didn't reply. That was unlike Francis, who rarely lacked for something to say. His face shifted and changed more than once, as if he struggled for words to express himself. "Arthur was raised to it," he muttered finally. "I haven't been. My life has been my own—I've made mistakes, done things I shouldn't have, and wouldn't have done if I'd known . . ."

"Haven't we all?" But it struck her that if they'd known about this all their lives, she wouldn't be a spinster now. If she'd been the sister of the Duke of Durham ten years ago, even just the sister to the heir presumptive, she would have had at least one suitor, at least one chance to find happiness and a home of her own. For a moment the thought made her throat constrict.

As if hearing her thoughts, her brother mustered a smile. "There's one good deed I may do because of this. I shall make you an heiress, Meg. You'll have a queue of suitors before the end of the month."

She should have known he would settle on that one tender subject. She waved one hand with a bittersweet smile. "It's much too late for that. No one will want me now."

"For a fat enough dowry, my dear, every unattached man in town will want you."

She raised her eyebrows. "Shall we hold an auction, then? Except instead of taking bids, you'll make them. 'What will you require, sir, to marry my sister? Five thousand pounds? Six?'"

"It will cost more than that, I expect." He ducked when she threw a pillow at him. "But don't you worry. You may help choose the fellow."

"From all the impoverished fortune hunters who will apply?

No, thank you." She made herself laugh. How like Fate to play such a cruel joke. Now that she was finally resigned to a spinster's life, men would line up at her door. The trouble was, none of them would want *her* any more than they had ten years ago; they would be lined up for Francis's money, and only marry her as the cost of getting it. Why couldn't she have found a simple country curate years ago, who would have taken her with only the five hundred pounds left to her in her father's will? That would have made this news a heaven-sent windfall.

"That's quite a number of men," Francis replied. "You'll like one of them, mark my words."

Margaret started to scoff, but saw his face. A cold breath of worry whispered over her skin; he had that set, determined expression she had learned to fear. "I don't want old Durham's money," she said, striving for lightness. "Give me only enough to tempt a country squire, and I shall be happy chasing his dogs from the garden and counting his silver. Anyone higher than that would be hopelessly pained by me, and I by him."

He turned to her, a hard light in his eyes. "Oh no. If I must be a duke, my sister shall be a lady. You'll have an enormous dowry, and take your pick of all the gentlemen in England. I don't wish to be married, but you do—you always have. And now you shall be."

She sat in silence. "I should have poisoned you years ago."

Francis laughed, his face relaxing until he looked more like his usual self. "And now you've missed your chance! No one would have missed Mr. Francis de Lacey, but they'll hang you for killing the Duke of Durham."

She thought back to the preening men who danced attendance on the wealthy young ladies. She had learned early on that money made a plain girl prettier, and enough money made an ugly girl beautiful. The thought of those conniving leeches calling on her now made her shudder in disgust, and she quietly resolved to have nothing at all to do with any man who only wanted money. "At the moment, I would gladly risk it."

CHAPTER TWO

London, 1771

"You're done for, Dowling. You really have no choice."

Rhys Corwen, sixth Earl of Dowling, clutched his decanter of whiskey to his chest and took a large swallow from his glass of the same. "Bugger off, Clyve."

Viscount Clyveden laughed. "Oh, come now. You'll have no one left if I go." He pushed his chair back on two legs and grinned at Rhys, who glared back. He wished Clyve would go and leave him alone to brood in misery. "Would you like a look at the list my mother made?"

"As if I'd take any of your leavings. It's always been the other way round, you know."

"These aren't leavings," said Clyve with a shudder. "These are potential brides—*brides*, man. I assure you, none of them are mine, and you are welcome to any of them. Or all of them."

Rhys gulped more whiskey, even though it was not having the intended effect. His goal was to become soundly, blessedly foxed, perhaps to the point of insensibility. Instead the liquor was only making his head pound like the devil, and Clyve, who refused to leave like the rest of his former friends, was gleefully chattering away when Rhys would have paid a fortune for silence.

Well—obviously he wouldn't pay a fortune. He didn't have one anymore. He had, in fact, virtually nothing that wasn't entailed or mortgaged three times over. The letters lying on the table clearly spelled out the dire nature of his circumstances, from the recent disaster at home in Wales to the depletion of his accounts in town. Even the whiskey was bought on credit he had no way to repay. The thought made him take another drink.

"My mother helpfully noted each lady's dowry," Clyve went on, taking out a paper and squinting at it. "Some of these chits would pull you right out of the River Tick." He whistled. "Especially this one. Good Lord. I might pay a call on her myself."

"I thought you didn't want any of them." But he leaned forward to pluck the list from Clyve's fingers.

"I never said I wanted her. But for forty thousand pounds I'll have a look."

Rhys read the name. "Margaret de Lacey. Who the devil is she? I've never heard of the de Laceys."

"You have," Clyve assured him. "The new Duke of Durham. This is his spinster sister."

Ah, *those* de Laceys. There had been a minor furor of gossip over the Durham title, passing as it did from the old duke, a tightfisted misanthrope who shunned society but was unquestionably of noble blood, to a distant great-nephew, a man almost in trade, if rumor could be believed. London was

divided between those who recoiled in horror at the prospect
of welcoming such a person into their midst—for an unmarried duke in possession of a large fortune must be welcomed,
no matter how uncouth he was—and those who awaited his
grand appearance with rabid anticipation of even more deli-
cious scandals and outrages to come. But the new duke wasn't
a young man, and no one would call his sister a spinster if she
were in her prime. Unmarried young women with forty thousand pounds were heiresses, not spinsters. "How old is she?" he
asked suspiciously.

Clyve shrugged. "Don't know. Does it matter?"

A bit. More than he was in any position to care about. Forty
thousand was immensely tempting, which made him wonder
how untempting the lady herself was. Rhys still clung to a little
pride, no matter how low his fortunes sank, and he really didn't
want a wizened shrew for a bride. He was the Earl of Dowling,
after all, not some mere baronet.

He studied the other names on the list. Lady Anne
Izard. Lady Charlotte Cranmore. Lady Phyllida Baverstock.
And Miss Margaret de Lacey, spinster relation of the Phi-
listine duke. "These are the ladies your mother wishes you
to marry?"

"Eh?" Clyve made a face. "She'd like me to court one of
them, at least. And if I'm to marry, I might as well get something out of it."

"Like forty thousand pounds," Rhys murmured. His eyes
traced the letters of her name. Pray God she was tolerable, and
not a prune-faced woman old enough to be his mother. That
could be even worse than a giggling chit of sixteen without two

thoughts in her brain. He tossed the list onto the table and leaned back again, closing his eyes. "I could flee to the colonies."

"And be murdered by savages? Good Lord, Dowling, you're not the first man to need money so badly he'll marry it."

"True." He stared up at the ceiling moodily. A long jagged crack split the plaster, threatening an ornate plaster cupid who clung to the cornice that circled the top of the walls. The cupid leered down at him, its grotesque grin mocking him from on high. His house was literally falling down around him, and Dowling Park, the seat of the earldom, was in even worse shape since the fire. He didn't have time to be particular about which heiress he married, not if he wanted to have an estate to save. "How bad can she be, really?" he asked, trying to persuade himself. "How bad could any of them be?"

"Precisely." Clyve rapped his knuckles on the arm of his chair. "Just choose one, get an heir or two on her, then send her off to the country and you'll never need see her again."

Rhys sighed. He supposed it was the best course open to him. It was certainly better than the alternatives, which included losing everything his ancestors had amassed and being locked away in the Fleet, if he couldn't manage to scarper off to the Continent. When viewed from that angle, marriage didn't look quite so bad. He set the decanter on the table with a clank. "Very well. I shall go courting."

Clyve grinned. "Knew you would. Mind if I come along?"

"To take your pick of my discards, as usual?" Rhys managed a cocky grin in reply. Perhaps if he brought Clyve along, it would seem like their typical jaunts, with nothing of sacrifice about it. One of the girls might turn out to be pretty, and it wouldn't be a punishment to bed her. And he only needed to do that once or twice, to make everything irrevocable. Then he could get on with the important duty, restoring his family fortunes and estate.

The first introductions were contrived with little effort. Clyve reported two young ladies would be at the Willoughby ball, so Rhys steeled himself to the task and unearthed his invitation. They encountered Lady Anne first. She was pretty, in a pale, thin way, and struck dumb with nerves at the sight of him. Rhys felt her hand tremble as he bowed over it, and the panicked look in her eyes made him think of a hare cornered by the hounds. He conversed politely with her mother, who was unquestionably pleased to make his acquaintance, and took his leave feeling like a sinner escaping Purgatory.

Lady Charlotte was also in attendance. She was more promising than Lady Anne, a pretty girl who responded very graciously when they were introduced. She was young, but appeared to have a bit of spirit and even some sense. Since she was also surrounded by several other gentlemen of rank, including some with fortunes of their own, Rhys foresaw stiff competition for the lady and her twenty-five thousand pounds. Still, he was confident in his title and his own personal persuasions, should he decide to set himself to winning her. He deemed Lady Charlotte possible.

"Very pretty," said Clyve as they walked away, sounding somewhat surprised. "Wonder how I was never introduced to her."

"If you like her," began Rhys, but Clyve threw up his hands.

"Well, I didn't say that! Only that one might take a second

look. I thought I knew every handsome lady in town, but I don't recall her." They passed through the ballroom back into the hall. Clyve glanced longingly toward the room opposite the ballroom, where plumes of smoke trailed out. Clyve had a weakness for cards, but Rhys wasn't in the mood this evening. He sent the footman for his things.

"Clyve, if you took a fancy to her, admit it. I shan't disparage you for being struck by a pretty girl, with or without a fortune." Rhys took his hat and ran one hand over his head before putting it on. Clyve, who ran more to the dandyish than he did, had persuaded him he must wear powder for these forays into society, and it made his head itch.

His friend followed him out to the carriage and stepped in behind him. He reclined on the opposite seat, one hand dangling elegantly over the head of his walking stick. "There is a great difference between being struck and being foolish."

"Not two days ago you told me it was prudent to be struck by a girl, pretty or otherwise, so long as she came with a plump dowry."

"Yes, Dowling, in your circumstance, it would be prudent." Clyve smiled wryly. "In mine, it would be merely foolish."

Rhys just looked out the window as the carriage jerked forward, rocking over the rutted street. Clyve wasn't nearly bankrupt, as he was. His mother might be nattering at him to marry and produce an heir, but Clyve had been ignoring her for most of his life, and there was no reason he should heed her now. He didn't need the money. A flirtation with Lady Charlotte Cranmore would only put him needlessly in danger of the parson's noose. Lord Cranmore would have him strung up in a fortnight if Clyve so much as leered at his daughter.

He, on the other hand . . . Rhys heaved a silent sigh. It wasn't so much marriage he objected to as the necessity. Even under better circumstances it would be time for him to find a wife; he had turned thirty already. His father waited until his forties to marry, and as a result Rhys had been only ten when he inherited his title. His mother was married again before he turned eleven, and Rhys hadn't seen her more than a dozen times since then, just brief visits between school terms until he took himself off to London for good. She lived with her husband in York, Rhys lived in London, and they hadn't met in years. How fortunate he was to have Clyve's mother providing guidance on choosing a bride, however inadvertently.

"The real question is," Clyve said, "do *you* like her?"

"She's lovely," Rhys murmured shortly. "Very suitable."

"Your enthusiasm takes my breath away."

"Excellent."

"I'm not the one you need to impress," Clyve reminded him. "A woman wants to be wooed, Dowling. Try not to look impatient to be away from her, as you did Lady Anne."

"I did wish to be away from her, but I rather think if I wanted her, I would get her for the asking." He paused, thinking. "The Cranmore girl would have to be pursued, I grant you."

"Hotly." Clyve looked wistful at the thought. "How unfortunate she's not for me. I haven't had a promising seduction in months."

"Who are the other candidates on your list?"

"Baverstock's eldest girl. My mother prefers her; she wrote me just the other day to extol the poor girl's singing voice." Clyve shuddered. "It astonishes me what women think important in a wife."

"And the other one," Rhys said, remembering. "The very rich one."

"Ah, yes, the Durham spinster. I heard of her the other day." His friend sat forward, his face lighting with the fiendish malice of a born gossip. "Quite old—thirty or more—and thin and plain as pudding. They say her brother settled a fortune on her in desperate hopes of being rid of her at last; she's been under his roof for several years."

Rhys pictured a dour, unattractive woman, accustomed to ruling a merchant household. Could he really install such a creature as the mistress of Dowling Park? "I daresay he will be, if he's truly given her forty thousand pounds."

Clyve laughed. "Without a doubt! For that price, someone will be willing to have her."

He thought of all the use he could make of forty thousand pounds. It was an absolute fortune, and would propel him clear out of debt and still leave a pretty penny. He could repair the house and Dowling Park, even improve it. Refurnish it. Perhaps the prospect of refitting Dowling Park would win the heiress's shriveled heart. The estate house had good lines and character, and was set in a beautiful landscape. It had once been called the prettiest estate in England. It was a far cry from that now, but if he could tear down the decrepit east wing and rebuild the ruined front, it would be a gem once again. His spirits rose. Yes, a managing older woman with little experience of society might embrace the challenge of restoring Dowling, and do a splendid job of it, if she had taste.

And all he had to do was charm her into marrying him, leaving spinsterhood to become the Countess of Dowling. How hard could that be?

Chapter Three

Despite her trepidation, Margaret began to like being the sister of a duke.

It was quite a change; no sooner had Francis formally ascended to the title than a horde of retainers descended on their modest house in Holborn, tramping through the rooms at all hours of the day and night. The neighbors protested. The housekeeper threw up her hands over the constant stream of visitors. Finally even Francis had enough. The late Duke of Durham had built an enormous mansion in Berkeley Square, still so new some rooms weren't completed, and within a month her brother sold his house and removed across town. Margaret felt a twinge of worry as they left behind the comfortable neighborhood and drove across town, a distance of hardly more than a couple of miles but crossing an unfathomable gulf between Miss Margaret de Lacey, penniless spinster, and Miss Margaret de Lacey, sister of a duke.

Once installed in Berkeley Square, her brother charged her with finishing his house. Tentatively at first, but with more and more confidence as she realized the nearly unbounded possibilities open to her with Francis's new fortune at her disposal, she chose furniture and paint colors, upholstery and carpets. She replaced china and draperies, pensioned off several elderly servants, and hired a bevy of new ones. She hardly saw her brother, closeted away as he was with his new estate managers and business agents and solicitors, but when their paths did cross, he assured her she was doing a splendid job on the house, and he reminded her of his vow, to see her married.

Margaret laughed at that. She knew Francis meant the suitor of her choice, subject to his approval. "I doubt there's a man in Europe who could please both me and my brother," she told Miss Cuthbert, the middle-aged lady of impeccable reputation hired to be her companion and teacher in the ways of high society. "At least when I had nothing, I had no one to please but myself."

Miss Cuthbert looked at her in shocked disapproval. Miss Cuthbert was the granddaughter of an earl, raised in elegant society from birth, and was routinely shocked by things Margaret said. "Every lady should wish to be married," she said with her slightly nasal drawl. "Especially every lady of good fortune."

No one should know better than Miss Cuthbert that wanting to be married didn't necessarily mean one would be married, but Margaret kept the thought to herself. "I do wish to be married," she assured her companion. "Just not to the first single man with empty pockets who asks me."

Miss Cuthbert looked down her long, narrow nose. "Naturally not," she said in freezing tones. "I shan't permit that."

Privately Margaret thought Miss Cuthbert would be far less discriminating than she would be. The older lady had made it clear she was something of a matchmaker, and her purpose was to see her charges well married within a year. Margaret glared suspiciously at her brother when Miss Cuthbert baldly announced that last goal, but Francis shrugged it off and said of course Miss Cuthbert wished to see her well married; overseeing a high-profile marriage would enhance her status as a desirable companion for unmarried ladies, ensuring her more income in the future. Margaret imagined how her own life would have been, at Miss Cuthbert's age, if Cousin Arthur hadn't died without a son. Playing matchmaker to nouveau riche heiresses seemed less objectionable after that.

And she most certainly was an heiress. Francis had settled an obscene amount of money on her, so much she gasped in shock when he told her. Even Miss Cuthbert blinked when she heard. But Francis had set his mind on it, and wouldn't reconsider.

"Don't even think of protesting," he told her. "It's not even a year's income. I've only just sorted out where all the funds come from, and where they go, but you're my only family, Meg, and you deserve to benefit from this unexpected turn even more than I do."

"Goodness." She fanned herself. "Is this a benefit, or a curse?"

He scowled, rifling through the papers on his desk in search of something. He never seemed to have a spare moment anymore, and when she wished to see him, she had to make an appointment with his secretary and go to his study. "Only you would ask that. You've given every indication of pleasure thus far."

She blushed. He meant her clothes. It had been years since

anyone cared how she looked, and as she grew older and settled in spinsterhood, her wardrobe had grown simple and even a bit dull. But now she was an heiress, with a companion hired specially to help her attract a good match, and suddenly Margaret found herself wearing the most deliciously fashionable clothing. Silk stockings instead of wool. Snug new corsets that made her deeply thankful she hadn't put on much weight since her debut. Beautifully draped and embroidered dresses that shimmered and glowed when she moved and made her feel like a princess from another world. Hand-painted *chiné* silks and Mechlin lace and shoes that sparkled with spangles and gilt embroidery. Miss Cuthbert declared the wardrobe vital to her new standing; Francis made no objection; and Margaret reveled in every scrap of silk and lace she purchased. Of all the changes wrought by Francis's new title, she liked the clothes the best.

"You promised me I would have my choice." She returned to the important point. Her new clothing was the wardrobe of a fashionable, eligible woman, meant to attract a husband, but she wasn't about to yield on that one all-important point. "You won't change your mind or try to change mine, now you've committed such a dowry to me?"

"No." He pulled out one paper with a grunt of satisfaction and leaned back in his chair to read it.

"Truly?" she pressed. The amount of the dowry took her breath away, and made her anxious. It was a staggering sum. Her brother was too keen a businessman to allow that much money to flow from his coffers without having some say in where it went. His grand promise that she would have her choice began to look more complicated than simply choosing from the line of gentlemen, penniless or otherwise, who would queue for her hand.

"For God's sake, Maggie," he snapped. "For forty thousand pounds I expect to have my choice of every bachelor in England. What has you so upset?"

She froze at his words, then turned a narrow glare on him. "*I* shall have the choice," she said carefully. "Surely you meant to say *I* shall have my choice of bachelors."

"That's what I said." He frowned at whatever he was reading.

"No, it isn't. You said *you* shall have your choice—which is precisely what has me so upset. Your money, your choice. I'd rather have nothing!"

He waved one hand in exasperation. "I won't let you marry a charlatan! I'm not a fool."

"But within those bounds, you won't overrule me?"

Francis gave a huff. "I won't overrule you! Just don't fall for a swindler or a seducer. I trust you have more sense than that, Maggie."

She smiled in relief. Once her brother gave his word, he never went back on it. "Of course I do."

Invitations had piled up from the moment Francis assumed the title, but they hadn't gone out thus far. Now Miss Cuthbert began directing Margaret which ones would be fitting places to make her first appearances as the Duke of Durham's sister, and Francis agreed to escort them to a few. Society must be curious to set eyes on these upstart de Laceys, he said, but Margaret had to admit she was curious to see this new society as well. When she'd been a young woman brought to London in hopes of acquiring some sophistication and a husband, they had mixed mostly with other families like theirs: genteel, modestly well off, vaguely "connected" without being important themselves. The dukedom had vaulted them to the rarified echelon of the very richest and noblest families, though. At first she worried she would feel out of place and gauche, but after the first few events, she realized that was foolish. Francis was right; her new dowry made her the most eligible lady in town, despite being nearly twice the age of other debutantes. She only sat out dances by choice. Whenever she was hungry or thirsty, two gentlemen begged the honor of fetching refreshment for her. No matter where she went, a gentleman, or two or ten, hovered at her elbow.

At first it was flattering—no girl who has been ignored can resist a little delight in being the focus of so much male attention—but quickly grew tedious, and finally irksome. The constant horde of suitors imposed a barrier between Margaret and every other lady in the room except Miss Cuthbert, who followed her with the keen eye of a jailor watching a prisoner on parole. Whatever interest other ladies might have had in being friendly seemed to evaporate once all the eligible gentlemen in the room rushed to surround her. Society was a lonely, dull place with no friends, Margaret thought. She felt a glimmer of sympathy for her brother's continued refusal to marry and his fear of being hounded by unmarried ladies hoping to become a duchess. Of course, he could go about marriage very directly, while she must wait for an appropriate man to approach her. And so far, not a one had.

"This is a bloody waste of time," she fumed behind her fan to Miss Cuthbert one particularly bad evening. Three gentlemen had clung to her side all evening until she finally announced she had turned her ankle and marched off to sit with the ladies who had no partners—the place where she had spent most of her evenings as a young lady, and which suddenly looked almost idyllically peaceful.

"Miss de Lacey, mind your tongue," said her companion sternly. "Genteel ladies do not use vulgar language."

Ballocks to that, she thought, but it wasn't worth angering Miss Cuthbert to say so out loud. Now that she had come out in society, Miss Cuthbert was more intensely determined than ever to make Margaret into a proper lady, or at least into enough of one to snare an eligible husband. No one was more dismayed than Margaret herself to discover it wouldn't be a romantic, tender process, but more of a hard-fought campaign, with tactical objectives and maneuvers to get the desired proposal. She had no interest in manipulating a man into offering for her. It was bad enough she would have to question and doubt any protestations of love a suitor made, in suspicion that his affections were mainly for her fortune.

"I'm ready to go home," she announced.

Miss Cuthbert's lips tightened, but she couldn't protest. Francis had explicitly told her she was an advisor only. "I shall send for the carriage, Miss de Lacey." She rose and made her way through the room.

"Good heavens, I thought she'd never go," said a bright voice from Margaret's other side. "Is she your keeper? Even my mother doesn't hover so oppressively."

She turned to regard the speaker in surprise. A lady a few years younger than she beamed back, lively blue eyes twinkling in her round face. Her hair was pulled into a fashionable coiffure, but its reddish color and wiry curls were still apparent under the powder and bows. She wasn't a very pretty girl, but she looked interesting. And friendly. Margaret smiled back, cautiously. "My companion."

Her neighbor made a face. "Almost as bad! At least you may order a companion about. It's the other way around with mothers. My mother was intolerable until Freddie finally proposed. That seemed to lift a great weight off her! Well, I suppose it lifted a great weight off us all, but I'm especially grateful Mama no longer feels the need to hover over me."

Margaret stared at her in fascination. "I see."

The lady's smile turned sympathetic. "Do you? I think you must. Once you have a fiancé, the rest of them will leave you in peace."

"I hope so," murmured Margaret. She hesitated. "I am Margaret de Lacey."

"I know! Everyone knows." The lady put her fingers over her mouth, not quite hiding her abashed grin. "You must be aware of it, but I do beg your pardon for saying so in such a crass manner. I am Clarissa Stacpoole, and I always say too much."

"It's a pleasure to meet anyone who will speak frankly," replied Margaret, instinctively liking Clarissa.

"Lud! I know." Clarissa rolled her eyes. "Much of it is fear. I thought I would have to sew my lips together to keep from saying the wrong thing when I first came out in society. But once I was betrothed, and Freddie assured me he likes the way I talk, I felt at liberty to speak as I wish. Perhaps once you choose a gentleman, it will be easier to talk freely."

Since choosing a gentleman to marry was looming as an excruciating chore in Margaret's mind at that moment, this sounded like a hollow hope. "Perhaps."

"Has anyone caught your eye?" Clarissa slid into the seat next to her. Her face alight, her blue eyes swept the room. "I vow, it must be quite a daunting prospect to have them all slavering after you."

She glanced warily at Clarissa, uncertainty whispering through her mind. Her new acquaintance seemed genuine and warm, but Margaret wasn't about to bare her heart to a stranger, not when Miss Cuthbert had drummed it into her head how curious everyone would be about her and how circumspect she must be, for her own reputation and her brother's. "I hardly know how to reply," she said. "I have only entered society."

Clarissa gave her a saucy look. "If you want to know anything, you have but to ask. Most of the eligible men didn't have the slightest interest in me, but I find them all fascinating, rather like the creatures in a menagerie. Thank goodness my Freddie is a good fellow. Some of the men in London are quite depraved."

"How do you know?" Margaret was torn between looking for Miss Cuthbert and leaving, and hearing all the scandalous gossip about the men who swarmed her. This was an alluring proposition. Miss Cuthbert would hardly reveal a man's objectionable side unless it was related to his station or connections.

"When you're unwanted, hardly anyone notices you," said Clarissa with brutal candor. "I hear everything, and no one minds because I'm no one of importance." She nodded toward Viscount Aston, who had kissed Margaret's hand the other night and complimented her fine eyes. "*He* once told Freddie I had the face of a bulldog and the mind of a goose. I suppose even the geese in London know he has the French pox. Any time a gentleman resorts to cosmetics, suspect the pox."

"Oh." Margaret tried not to wipe her hand on her skirts. She took one look down at the pale pink silk, embroidered with silver rosettes on the stomacher and underskirt, and the urge passed. This gown was her favorite, and even if it were not, the silk alone had cost seventy pounds. It was as much as she'd spent on clothing in a year, before Francis inherited. "My companion neglected to offer that advice."

"Well, she probably considers him eligible. A very old title, you know, and a beautiful estate."

"He must be in want of money," said Margaret, eyes fixed straight ahead. "Everyone presented to me is."

Clarissa laughed, a full jolly sound. "I can't think of more than four or five peers who aren't! And one of them is your brother. Even those with a healthy income would always welcome more, and the easiest way to get it is to marry it." She inhaled sharply. "But no one is more in want than *he*."

Margaret followed her new friend's gaze, which had grown alert and intense. As soon as she found the focus of Clarissa's interest, though, it was apparent why. The man across the room was like a shade of night come into the glittering ballroom. He wore a suit of dark blue, which only made his swarthy skin darker above the white ruffle of his linen. His hair was brushed back and neatly queued, but unpowdered; a dark blot among all the wigs and powdered coiffures around him. His profile was strong, even fierce, with a sharp blade of a nose and a square chin. He smiled at something his companion said, and a slash of dimple appeared in his cheek. He looked like she had always imagined the Barbary pirates might, which was both fascinating and alarming.

"Who is he?" she whispered.

Without taking her eyes from him, Clarissa leaned closer. "The Earl of Dowling. He's utterly ruined; a flood swept away all his sheep, or some such thing, although how a man can be ruined by dead sheep, I'm sure I don't know. Oh, I hate to say it, but he's looking this way." She turned to Margaret and grasped her hand. "Of course you don't know me, but I would recommend great care with him. He is certainly looking for a wealthy bride, but he's a bit untamed. One of those Welsh, you know."

Margaret's jaw firmed. That was all she needed to know. Lord Dowling was indeed watching her with a possessive expression as he wound his way through the crowd toward her. In her younger years, as a hopeful, somewhat naive, young lady, she would have been tongue-tied with excitement at the approach of such a man. Tonight she felt her patience fray and finally snap. What a lark, that a man as handsome as sin itself would be strolling toward her with purposeful intent. She'd had enough of fortune hunters. Francis could keep his money, and Miss Cuthbert could find another victim for her machinations.

He came to a halt in front of her. Another man was with him, unnoticed until now, but he stepped forward and bowed with a great flourish. "Miss Stacpoole," he said to Clarissa with a wide smile. "How delightful to see you again."

"I would wholeheartedly repay your compliment, sir, if we had ever met before," said Clarissa, much to Margaret's hidden glee.

A flicker of consternation crossed the fellow's face. Margaret could tell he was a Society fribble of the highest order, possibly even one of what Miss Cuthbert disparagingly called "those macaronis," from his glittering shoe buckles to the exquisite lace that tumbled over his hands at his cuffs. The embroidery on his waistcoat alone put her beautiful new gown to shame. "Have we not met? Surely I could not have imagined it. I distinctly recall congratulating Mr. Eccleston on his betrothal to you, and toasting your upcoming marriage."

"Oh!" exclaimed Clarissa. "You know Freddie? Well, that is near enough to knowing me. How do you do, sir?"

"Very well," said the man with a mixture of relief and amusement. "I am Lord Clyveden. But I have brought my friend, Lord Dowling, who most particularly wished to be presented to you and your companion."

Lord Dowling bowed. There was no froth of lace spilling from his cuffs and his shoe buckles were plain, but he drew the eye far more than his glamorous friend. "Good evening," he said in a slightly raspy voice edged with a trace of accent.

It irked Margaret how much she liked his voice. He even sounded as she imagined a Barbary pirate would sound, just before he ravished a maiden. She lifted her chin and nodded regally to him. Miss Cuthbert would probably expire in despair that she hadn't risen and given a proper curtsey to an earl, but she was beyond caring. And where was Miss Cuthbert anyway? How long did it take to summon the bloody carriage?

"May I present Miss Margaret de Lacey," Clarissa was saying. "It is a great pleasure to make your acquaintance, my lord. Are you also friends with Freddie?"

His gaze hadn't left Margaret. "I have not the honor, Miss

Stacpoole," he replied. "I confess, I shamelessly forced Clyveden to introduce me so I might beg a dance of Miss de Lacey."

Her temper, never meek or quiescent, overshot its bounds. He thought she would fall into his penniless grip like an overripe plum. Ten years ago he wouldn't have noticed her if she'd flung herself naked in front of him. For the first time she realized Francis's money had reversed the usual positions: Before, she was the item for sale by marriage, and now she was the buyer. She looked him up and down, as one might inspect a horse for sale. "Completely destitute, are you?" she asked coolly.

His face froze, his dark eyes blank with surprise. Lord Clyveden made a strange choking sound. Even Clarissa's eyes widened. Margaret didn't care, and over Lord Dowling's shoulder, she saw Miss Cuthbert returning at last, a worried set to her grim features. She got to her feet, righteously ready to cut one vulture off before he got started. "You're the third earl to ask me to dance tonight. One trampled my shoes and the other hardly knew the steps, so I don't think I shall risk a third try. I hear you lost all your sheep, which is very sad for the sheep, but I don't consider myself a suitable replacement for any flock. My brother told me I shall have my choice of suitors, and I think it only sporting to tell you now that I shan't choose you, no matter how many people you coerce into presuming upon slight acquaintances with my friends for an introduction. In fact, I have recently decided I won't marry at all this year, or even next, so unless you have a reserve supply of goats or cows to tide you through a very long and arduous courtship, I suggest you seek your dancing partners among the more available heiresses."

She turned to her new friend, who regarded her with slack-jawed awe. "Good evening, Clarissa. I hope to see you again soon." And she turned on her heel and walked away, waving Miss Cuthbert toward the door as she went.

Rhys watched her go. He hadn't said more than "Good evening" to her, and she tore him to shreds. Her blue eyes blazed with scorn as she looked him over as if he were a maggoty side of beef, and she walked away from him and Clyve without so much as a curt nod of farewell. She strode through the ballroom as regally as any queen, twitching her lavishly embellished skirts from side to side to avoid crushing them, and people fell out of her way with bowed heads. He'd never seen the like.

Lady Charlotte the pursuable heiress was forgotten; so too was any thought of even meeting the other lady on Clyve's list. Miss de Lacey wasn't a beautiful, biddable girl. She was something else: a woman of passion and spirit with a sharp, bold wit, and even without forty thousand other charms, Rhys would have felt the pull.

"A reserve supply of goats!" Clyve was almost strangling on his laughter. "Great God! What an introduction!"

"Yes, indeed," he murmured, his mouth beginning to curl in anticipation. "And by God, she's the one I want."

CHAPTER FOUR

Miss Cuthbert was not pleased she had dismissed the Earl of Dowling, but Margaret said he'd been impertinent and that ended the discussion. She felt a bit of shame impugning the earl when in all fairness he had done no more than ask her to dance, but mostly she was so relieved to have one less avaricious suitor, the feeling was easy to ignore. The entire matter was soon forgotten, as Miss Cuthbert secured an invitation to the Countess of Feithe's spring garden party. Margaret wasn't sure it was such a triumph as her companion presented it, since the invitation was really to Francis, but Miss Cuthbert assured her it was one of the finest events in the London Season, and the very cream of society would be in attendance. It was quite astonishing how their lives had changed. She had never met a duke before her brother became one, and now Miss Cuthbert swore she would be presented to three this very day.

Lord Feithe had built an impressive estate on the western edges of town, almost to Chelsea. They went by boat, as it turned out the Durham estate included a small yacht. Margaret caught her brother's eye as they traveled upriver, but he just grinned and strode off to stand by the helm and direct the captain. Of all the inherited riches and responsibilities of Durham, it was clear Francis liked the yacht best.

"I beg you to remember your dignity today," said Miss Cuthbert. Her face was as white as the foam plowed up by the bow of the boat, slicing through the murky waters.

Margaret lifted her face to the stiff breeze, keeping her dainty chip bonnet from flying off with one hand. Francis was right about the yacht; she liked it, too. Perhaps if Miss Cuthbert would close her eyes and enjoy the breeze, she wouldn't look so sickly. "Of course," she murmured. "When have I forgotten it?"

"This is—this is a very important invitation," replied the woman with an audible gulp. "One breach of etiquette will mean—mean you are not invited back."

"I'm only invited because everyone is so wild with curiosity to see Francis. As long as he is unmarried and willing to accompany me, I doubt I shall be in want of invitations." Margaret glanced at the older woman. "Miss Cuthbert, do sit down. You look quite green."

"You are too careless," insisted Miss Cuthbert, clinging stubbornly to the rail. Margaret edged a step away, not wanting to risk her crisp skirts if her companion should become violently ill. "Gentlemen care for more than just a lady's dowry."

Margaret faced the breeze and said nothing. Did they truly? Miss Cuthbert meant her demeanor and bearing, her ability to play a proper lady, but Margaret wanted more than that. Did the men she met care for her thoughts, her feelings, her hopes? They certainly hadn't shown much interest in any part of her before she had a fortune. She didn't blame Miss Cuthbert, who was only trying to bring her out in society as promised. But she was no longer the starry-eyed girl who longed so fiercely to be sought after, courted, and married. She was old enough to have seen unhappy marriages, contracted with amorous or avaricious speed and repented until death parted them. Living on her brother's charity was a far sight better than being wed to a man who wanted only her money. Marriage might last a lifetime, but money did not.

"I promise I shall be the very picture of grace and charm," she said at last. "I shan't humiliate you, Miss Cuthbert."

"Do not be ridic—" The boat hit a swell and the prow rose unexpectedly before dropping with a tremendous splash. Margaret caught her breath with excitement at the sudden feeling of lightness inside her, Miss Cuthbert went white and folded herself over the rail, and behind them both Francis laughed.

"An apt preparation for the day's events, Miss Cuthbert," he shouted. "I feel quite the same way!"

They reached the landing soon after, and Margaret put her arm around Miss Cuthbert as the poor woman staggered up the stairs to the broad terrace. Once on dry land again she recovered quickly and resumed her air of command, rather unfortunately in Margaret's opinion. But then, she supposed Miss Cuthbert would force herself off her deathbed to present a good front at Lord Feithe's famous garden party. In spite of herself she was curious, and even a tiny bit hopeful.

It turned out to be much the same as every other society gathering she had attended, though, with the sole saving grace of being set outside in a lovely park on a beautiful day. Francis, the lout, took one look at the beaming, breathless throng of ladies awaiting his arrival and decamped to the house, no doubt intending to hide away in the smokiest corner until it was time to go. Miss Cuthbert, on the other hand, refused to leave her side, hovering at her elbow and murmuring information about each gentleman's prospects and family until Margaret had enough. She stared down her companion, announced she was going for a solitary stroll, and slipped out of the garden by dodging into a row of hemlocks.

Outside the confines of the formal garden, it was quiet. Some of the breeze from the river swept up the lawns, and she breathed deeply of it. Up river from London, the air was fresh and crisp, free of the stench of tanneries, slaughterhouses, and sewers. It reminded her of her childhood home, far from London but blessedly devoid of fortune hunters as well.

She strolled along a gravel path, glad for a peaceful walk. Heiresses and sisters of dukes weren't allowed nearly as much freedom to go out alone as ordinary spinsters were. She wished Clarissa Stacpoole was in attendance, but so far she hadn't seen her. Clarissa might be impertinent and gossipy, but it was a great deal more interesting to talk to her than to Miss Cuthbert or any of the would-be suitors who trailed after her. Margaret thought of her long-standing friends from Holborn, and felt caught, lonely and isolated, in the chasm between her old life and her new.

Lost in thought, she didn't see the man on the path until she almost walked into him. She stopped short. "I beg your pardon, sir."

"Not at all, Miss de Lacey." He bowed as his voice resonated in her blood. She remembered that voice. It was the poor earl she had verbally thrashed the other night, just for asking her to dance.

Stiffly she dropped a curtsey. "I did not mean to intrude, my lord. Pray excuse me."

"On the contrary," he said as she started to go back the way she'd come. "I was hoping to meet you again." She darted a wary glance at him. He was watching her with darkly amused eyes and a slight smile curving his mouth. The breeze caught the black bow at his nape and fluttered the ends over his broad shoulders. Today he wore lighter colors, a moss green coat of fine wool over an ivory waistcoat and breeches, but it didn't make him appear any less pirate-like. Perhaps even the contrary. There was something very intriguing about an untamed man in the veneer of a civilized gentleman. "Perhaps this time I might improve your opinion of me."

Margaret felt again the prickle of discomfort at the way she had abused him. "I'm not in such an ill temper today," she said. "I must beg your pardon for making light of your sheep tragedy."

He dipped his head. "Thank you for the condolences."

She hesitated. "How many died?"

"Almost five thousand head." She gasped. "It was a flood," he added. "A sudden torrential rain. They were caught in a valley, and would not run uphill despite the herders' efforts."

"And none were saved?"

"Not many. Sheep aren't the cleverest creatures." He raised his eyes to the heavens wearily. "Bloody idiots, really."

She laughed before she could stop herself, and then tried to mask it with a cough as Lord Dowling cocked his head and quirked his lips. "I hope you didn't expect more of sheep."

"No. I wish I'd had the benefit earlier of your suggestion to invest in goats or cows."

"Perhaps you should keep them all out of valleys, just to be safe."

He laughed. Margaret smiled in reply, then realized what she was doing and wiped it from her face. He was acting so warmly because he wanted to marry an heiress, she reminded herself. "I must return," she said, her voice stilted. "Your pardon, sir."

His eyes glinted at her. "So you can suffer the importunate attentions of other destitute gentlemen?"

She raised her chin. "I'm sure it isn't any of your concern what I intend to do. I was wrong to be so curt the other night, but you and I are strangers still. Good day, my lord."

"We won't be strangers for long," he said with that trace of amusement that irked her so.

"Did you not listen to what I said the other night? My brother has given me the choice." She couldn't resist looking him up and down once more, although without the chilly scorn she had managed the first time they met. Had she really been so quick to dismiss such a dangerously attractive man? He was one of the many fortune hunters chasing her, true, but he was the handsomest one of the pack. From his splendidly muscular calves to the dark waves of his hair, he was utterly beautiful.

"I heard you." He came closer, his shoes crunching on the gravel of the path. Margaret kept her face smooth and composed, but she couldn't make her feet move and walk away. The nerve of him! To stand there caressing her with his gaze as if he wanted *her*—her, not her money. It was shocking and impudent and rude and . . . and . . . and somewhat thrilling. Which was even worse than rude, she was sure.

"But what you didn't allow for, my dear," he went on softly, "was that you'll choose me."

What nerve he had! "I am quite familiar with the concept of impossibility," she snapped back. "I refuse to marry any man who needs money."

"No, you're going to marry me." He lowered his eyelashes and gave her a wicked smile. "And we'll be very happy."

She stared at him for a moment. In spite of her outrage, something inside her hummed like a barely plucked string at his tone, deep and rough and tinged with the promise of something so sinfully pleasurable . . . she couldn't even imagine it. She didn't *want* to imagine it. "You'd swear the same to any heiress. They say you're utterly ruined."

"Not ruined. Destitute. There's a difference." He held up one finger as she started to speak again. Somehow he had moved close enough to touch her, as he did now, laying that bare finger against her lips. "But we're the same sort. We belong together."

She jerked away from him. Her lips tingled from the touch, and it was all she could do not to lick them. "I fear lunacy has overtaken you, sir."

He laughed, a low, easy rumble that made her heart skip a beat. "Undoubtedly! That doesn't change the truth of my statement, though. We're two of a kind, you and I."

She sniffed. "Good day, Lord Dowling. Take care on your way back to Bedlam."

"We neither of us arrived at our current circumstances through our own actions," he called out as she walked away. "You're an heiress through the fortunate providence of Arthur de Lacey's death without issue." She whirled to face him, mouth open in fury, but he only nodded as he strolled after her. "I'm on the brink of ruin because my father, and then his appointed guardian, thought our family fortunes lay in the colonies. Unfair in both cases, don't you agree?"

She found her voice. "I never asked to be an heiress. I told my brother to keep his money. The ducal branch of the family cut us off decades ago. How dare you imply I reveled in the death of—"

"Of a cousin you never met, and probably would have disliked if you had." He grinned again. "I knew him in passing. He would have been just like his father, miserly with his patronage and cruel to his servants. No one in England was sorry to see him meet an untimely end." He paused. "Although I do believe he was near sixty. Hardly cut down in the blush of youth."

"I never knew him, and didn't realize until after his untimely death what it meant for my brother," she said coldly. "I was happy as I was!"

"Were you?" His gaze wandered down her bare throat and bosom, over her tightly laced bodice, past her striped silk petticoat, all the way to her embossed red leather shoes tied with jaunty black ribbons. Margaret had never felt so studied, and even though her face flushed at his impertinence, some small, wicked part of her liked it. If he was merely pretending to find her attractive, he was doing a very flattering job of it.

Which was ridiculous. He would say anything to seduce her, and once she succumbed to his charm and married him, he could lock her away in his attics and spend every last farthing of Francis's money.

"I *was* happy," she told him with hard finality. "I had dear friends—who now are too inferior for me to associate with, for all their kindness and good natures. I had a comfortable home—not a mansion, but warm and safe and cozy. I was never hungry, or cold, or despised."

"But did you ever have passion?" he murmured. "A lover? A husband to protect and provide for you, to hold you in his arms at night, to give you children?"

The charge struck home, but she hid her flinch. "One doesn't need those things, my lord."

"No?" He arched a brow. "Perhaps some do not . . . most likely because they don't know what they're missing. But you, my dear, you need them. You crave them. If you didn't, you wouldn't be strolling Lord Feithe's grounds wearing a dress worth more than a farmer makes in a year. You're disgusted by me, and every other man simpering over you, because you want someone who will love you, not your dowry."

He was right, sadly. Her shoulders hurt from the effort of keeping still. "You wouldn't even be speaking to me if not for that dowry," she said softly.

"Only because I never had the chance to meet you before."

That made her laugh. "Indeed? You would have called us two of a kind when I was merely the sister of a businessman in Holborn, years past her prime with only five hundred pounds to her name?"

"No, I would have said you were above me," he replied with a remarkably straight face. "I inherited my title twenty years ago, and there was precious little money in the estate then. I was only a boy of ten; a cousin of my father's had the management of all that was mine until I reached twenty-one, and he did a piss-poor job of it. I watched my inheritance bleed away because he fancied everything would be solved by tobacco farms in the colonies." His voice was growing tight, but he lifted his shoulders and his tone eased. "Perhaps it did, until the slave rebellion, followed by the fire, and then fever. Now the colonists are agitating against British rule, and the land isn't worth a quarter what he paid for it."

"You'd better sell it then, and cut your losses," she said tartly.

He extended his arms, palms up. "I did. It took two years and cost me dearly, but I promptly invested the proceeds in a flock of Cheviot—a respectable, reliable English way for a gentleman to support himself. Very nice wool, you see. If only they could swim. And now, as you said the other night, I'm completely destitute, brought low by a cursed weed and idiotic sheep."

One of their neighbors in Holborn had been ruined when his warehouse burned. It could happen just as easily to an earl, she supposed. She cleared her throat. "I am very sorry for it, just as I'm sorry I lost my temper. But that doesn't make us alike."

"But I want what you want, my dear," he said softly, gliding a step closer. She tried to meet his eyes without tilting back her head, and couldn't do it. "I want a wife to hold me in her arms at night. To give me children. To find the sort of passion and companionship that lasts a lifetime."

Oh goodness. She swallowed, telling herself she was insulted and outraged instead of alive with longing at the images he conjured. "Very prettily said, sir, but it won't persuade me to marry you. I hope you didn't expect it would. Good day."

His low laugh floated after her as she turned and walked away. "This wasn't persuasion, darling," he said. "But next time we meet . . . it will be."

Chapter Five

Rhys followed her at a leisurely pace. She was aware of his presence; twice he caught her stealing glances over her shoulder at him. Each time she immediately snapped her head forward and walked a bit faster, her spine stiff—with outrage, he presumed. Her blond curls, pinned up under an absurd little hat, bobbed sharply with each step she took, and her skirts swayed with appealing vigor. He enjoyed the sight. He liked picturing her hips swaying like that without the concealment of a hoop and petticoat. Everything about her was intriguing.

Clyve met him at the edge of the party. Technically Rhys hadn't been invited to this gathering, but Clyve appealed to Lady Feithe, his one-time lover, and persuaded her the notorious Earl of Dowling wouldn't cause a stir at her party. And Rhys wouldn't. He'd only come today to verify his initial impression of the lady, and begin his courtship if circumstances permitted. It had been a complete surprise when she came around the path alone, but a welcome one. It took only a few minutes for him to know, with an unearthly sort of certainty and calm, she was the woman he wanted. Life would never be dull with her. She had a retort to everything he said, and she made him laugh, even about the death of his sheep, a subject that invariably roused his temper whenever anyone else mentioned it.

And to his everlasting relief, she was quite attractive. Her face lacked the soft, girlish plumpness of Lady Charlotte's, but he had no objection to that. She was a woman, not a girl, and Rhys had always found women far more appealing than girls. She was slender and tall for a woman, with a lovely bosom very temptingly displayed today by her tightly laced bodice. He had admired her spirit the other night, but today he realized her physical charms were considerable as well.

Yes, she was the one for him. All he had to do was persuade her he was the man for her.

"How did you get on?" Clyve asked. "I've been quite beside myself with anticipation, imagining all manner of seduction."

"That's my future countess. Mind your tongue." Rhys watched her hurry through the crowd until she reached the side of her austere companion. Miss Cuthbert, he remembered, doubtless some connection of the Earl of Islington. From the safety of her dragon's side, Miss de Lacey peered back at him once more. Rhys smiled and bowed politely. Her defiant expression faded into annoyance, and then she gave him her back once more, slipping further into the crowd of guests. He chuckled.

"I see you've won her heart already." Clyve grinned, watching the exchange. "When shall the wedding be?"

"Idiot," said Rhys absently. "I haven't proposed yet." The lady from the other night, Miss Stacpoole, had joined Miss de Lacey. Were they truly friends? They made a decidedly unusual pair: short, plump Miss Stacpoole with her frizzy red hair and unfortunate nose, and willowy Miss de Lacey with her glossy blond curls and pert pink mouth that cried out to be kissed—soon, if he had anything to say about it. "Her friend," he said to Clyve. "You're acquainted with her?"

Clyve snorted. "Not at all, as you saw the other evening. I know her fiancé, though. Viscount Eccleston's heir. Genial chap; not very bright. She shall lead him like a mule on a rope."

Margaret de Lacey wouldn't lead him, but neither would she be a meek, quiet wife. Rhys foresaw a future filled with passions of all sorts, and took a long, deep breath to quiet the unexpected urge to whisk her away to begin courting her in earnest. That would be foolish. She wasn't a girl who would be impressed by his title or easily bowled over by a little charm. She would need persuading. Pursuing. Tempting.

"Introduce me to young Mr. Eccleston," he said to Clyve. "I have a feeling he and I are going to be friends."

"The Earl of Dowling is watching you, Margaret," Clarissa reported in a loud whisper.

Margaret set her teeth and led the way to the pavilion set up to shade the ladies from the sun. "Does he still have that arrogant smile on his face?"

Clarissa craned her neck. Margaret started to tell her not to be obvious, but refrained. Lord Dowling knew they were aware of his interest. He'd been looking at her every time she happened to glance his way, which she had done an unfortunate number of times. Was he still watching her? She thought slightly better of him after their brief meeting on the path, but his parting threat to persuade her to marry him still echoed in her ears. He wanted her money, she reminded herself again, even though he looked as if he wanted something else from her entirely. Much to Margaret's disgust, she found she wasn't immune to the temptation when her eyes met his, so dark and intent, his wicked mouth touched with a smile that promised all sorts of pleasures. Better that Clarissa be obvious than she. Especially since Margaret really wanted to know.

"Yes," her friend said after a moment. "He looks quite impertinent. Good heavens, a gentleman ought to know better than to look at a lady that way in public, especially a lady he hardly knows. Of course, everyone knows he really isn't a gentleman—the Welsh are quite, quite wild, I hear—but his rude friend ought to tell him. People will notice!"

As if to prove Clarissa's point, Miss Cuthbert hurried after them. "Miss de Lacey," she said sternly, "I must ask, what occurred on your stroll? Did you meet anyone?"

She breathed deeply to control her temper. "Why do you ask, Miss Cuthbert?"

Her companion moved closer, eyeing Clarissa with resignation. She dropped her voice even lower. "A gentleman is staring at you with the most improper expression! And he arrived from the same direction you returned, only shortly after you!"

"I did not have an assignation with anyone," she said shortly. "I chanced to meet the Earl of Dowling as I walked, but our conversation was brief and unremarkable." Except for the way he made her laugh, and the way his gaze felt like a physical touch on her skin. "I cannot help it if someone is staring at me in any manner. If it disturbs you, perhaps you should tell him to stop."

Miss Cuthbert grew rigid with disapproval. "It is hardly my place to do such a thing." It was probably Francis's place, Margaret supposed, but he wouldn't be dragged out of the safety of Lord Feithe's smoking room just to tell some brash earl to stop staring at her. Francis, in fact, would probably be all in favor of it, and go tell Dowling to make an offer for her.

"Then it seems a hopeless case. The only way I can make him stop looking at me is to leave, and I thought we were to stay for dinner."

Miss Cuthbert closed her eyes in despair. "Miss de Lacey," she said plaintively. "You must have a care for your standing!"

"I don't think it will hurt her much to have Lord Dowling watch her," said Clarissa. "Everyone is well aware of what he wants, but really, if one must be pursued by fortune hunters, at least Dowling is young and handsome."

"Young and handsome do not make an eligible match," snapped Miss Cuthbert.

"He's also an earl, and Mama tells me his property used to be one of the loveliest in England." Clarissa shrugged good-naturedly when Margaret looked at her in surprise. "Mama had these wild, foolish ideas at one time. She had a list of every unmarried man in England, detailing advantages and disadvantages. Every night I say a prayer of thanks Freddie saved me before she could grow desperate and start pushing me into carriages with them."

"Surely she wouldn't have," exclaimed Margaret.

Clarissa gave her a speaking look. "I hadn't enough money for Dowling in any event. My father would have kept Mama from throwing me at him, just because Papa appreciates a well-laid table and Dowling is at his last farthing. Papa never would have been able to visit if I'd been Lady Dowling, making do with mutton and fish for dinner. Not that I would have minded, just once, seeing how ruthless and barbaric those Welshmen can be . . ."

"Miss Stacpoole!" Miss Cuthbert was turning purple. "Remember yourself!"

Clarissa pressed her lips together and made a face behind the older woman's back. Margaret choked back a laugh. "What is so wrong with Lord Dowling, Miss Cuthbert?" she asked on impulse. From the corner of her eye she could see him, together with his peacock of a friend from the other night. That one glittered in the sunlight, with silver embroidery covering his sleeves to the elbow, while Lord Dowling's unadorned coat was almost austere in comparison, but somehow the contrast made him seem more masculine. More approachable. More like someone she would know and like. Try as she might, she couldn't forget what he said about them being alike in some way.

Perhaps she had been a bit hard on Lord Dowling. None of her other suitors would be so brash as to admit they needed money; they preferred to pretend a sudden interest in her eyes or lips. No one had told her so bluntly he had something she craved as well: love, passion, friendship. Margaret wasn't a nobleman's daughter, raised from birth knowing her marriage would be a business transaction between families rather than a personal affinity between man and woman. Her parents had loved each other, and deep down, Margaret admitted she expected both more and less from marriage than Miss Cuthbert assumed. Less, in that she didn't require a certain rank in a prospective husband, but more, in that she did require true affection—even love, if possible. She was exasperated by Miss Cuthbert's favored suitors because they had impeccable dignity and rank, but little chance of engaging her interest, let alone her affections. Lord Dowling was the only one who even claimed he would try. She doubted he would succeed, but perhaps ... just perhaps ... she was a little curious how he planned to go about it.

"His entire life has been a scandal, Miss de Lacey," said Miss Cuthbert in answer to her question. "That is all you need to know."

Margaret glanced at Clarissa. "What sort of scandal?"

Her companion looked down her nose. "It is unseemly to discuss it." Behind her, Clarissa's eyes were twinkling brightly, and she winked.

Margaret smiled. "Very well. I wouldn't wish to be unseemly." Not when Clarissa was so clearly willing to discover and tell her everything she wanted to know. She took Miss Cuthbert's arm. "Let us return to the party. I promise to observe every stricture of modest and decent behavior from now on."

But only for today.

CHAPTER SIX

Frederick Eccleston was much as Clyve described him. Middling tall with a head of bushy brown hair that resisted powdering with impressive tenacity, he was an easy, amiable fellow a little younger than Rhys. When Clyve introduced them, Rhys made a great effort not to say anything at all of his interest in Margaret de Lacey, but Eccleston appeared impervious to any shade of subtlety. He liked to talk, and it took only a question or two to spawn a rambling discourse on everything he knew of the subject.

Clarissa Stacpoole, Rhys learned, was inclined to gossip more than she should. Eccleston was very fond of his fiancée, but freely admitted her weaknesses. "O' course all women talk," he explained in his Yorkshire drawl. "Clarissa can chatter them all into the grave. Her mama tried to tell me it was nerves, but I know better. Known her since she was a girl, and she's been the same. If Clarissa hears something interesting, she has to tell someone."

"Even if sworn to secrecy?" Rhys asked in amusement.

Eccleston paused, looking surprised. "I don't know. Never tried asking."

Rhys told himself to speak cautiously in front of Miss Stacpoole. "I ask because I find it hard to believe she would share confidences from her friends."

"Now, that's fair to say." The other man nodded. "Once she takes up friends with someone, she's devoted. Say one word against her younger brother and she'll skewer you through the gut."

"She appeared quite devoted to you when I met her."

Eccleston grinned in pride. "Did she? Clarissa's a good girl. I expect we'll get on well enough after the wedding."

That sounded like a rather modest goal, but he soberly wished Eccleston the very happiest of futures. Every man must be allowed his own version of paradise, and if Eccleston wished only an amiable contentment, so be it.

For himself, though, Rhys wanted more. He had quite forgotten his reluctance to pay court to any heiress because Margaret de Lacey was no ordinary heiress. *I was happy as I was*, she had told him, and he believed her. Her father had been a gentleman, but of much more modest circumstances than those she now enjoyed. Rhys had heard enough gossip about the de Laceys' sudden good fortune to know she and her brother weren't being welcomed with open arms by everyone among the nobility. Since he knew first hand how quickly and capriciously society could turn on a person, changing from indulgent to disdainful in the blink of an eye, he realized how awkward her position was: If she kept up her old friendships, her new society would never accept her, but the size of her dowry isolated her from noblewomen who might have become her new friends. Until she married, Miss de Lacey would no doubt find herself rather lonely.

And she wasn't meant to be alone. She blushed when he commented on her reasons for wearing so fashionable a gown, and he caught the flicker of pain in her eyes when he asked if she didn't want passion in her life. He meant everything he told Margaret at Lord Feithe's: He wanted more from her than her money. Far from his original reluctance to meet any heiresses, he had leapt straight to wanting Margaret herself. A sensible, clear-eyed, attractive woman who longed for passion—and in possession of forty thousand pounds. It was beginning to appear Divine Providence itself had directed him to her.

Accordingly he wasted no time the next evening in approaching the lady, once more found with her friend and Mr. Eccleston. "Good evening, Miss Stacpoole, Miss de Lacey. Eccleston." He bowed to each lady.

"Good evening, Lord Dowling." Miss Stacpoole looked at him with amused curiosity. Miss de Lacey eyed him with cool suspicion and said nothing. "Freddie, I didn't know you were acquainted with His Lordship."

"And why not?" replied Eccleston, to Rhys's surprise. "We're both Emmanuel man."

"Quite right," he said easily. How fortunate Eccleston had been in his own college at Cambridge. "And I shall presume upon on it. Miss Stacpoole, may I beg the honor of a dance?"

Margaret, who had braced herself for that very question, blinked. Clarissa's eyes opened wide, and she stared at the earl without blinking. Oh, he was a canny one, she thought in irritation. He wasn't even looking at her, his attention fixed on poor Clarissa, who had gone as pale as snow beneath her freckles. Margaret remembered all her friend's ruminations about how wild a Welshman might be, and wondered if Clarissa was truly frightened.

"Er . . . Yes, sir." Clarissa's voice was higher than usual as she bobbed a clumsy curtsey and laid her hand in Dowling's waiting palm. "Freddie . . ." She looked at her fiancé in mute appeal.

"Go on," he said with a good-natured smile. "I trust Dowling—but I'll be waiting right here, eh?"

"Of course." Smiling nervously, Clarissa let Lord Dowling lead her to join the dance without a glance backward. The earl didn't look back, either, and Margaret caught sight of that slashing dimple of his as he said something to Clarissa.

"I expect I'll never hear the end of this," said Mr. Eccleston at her side, watching them. "Heaven help me if Dowling's a better dancer than I. Would it be wrong of me to hope he treads on her toe?"

Margaret snapped open her fan. "As long as you wish for him to tread lightly on her toe, I see no harm in it." Eccleston laughed. For a moment they stood in silence, watching the dancers step through the elegant minuet. To her disgust, the Earl of Dowling appeared to be a fine dancer.

"Are you old friends with Lord Dowling?" she asked, telling herself it was to make conversation, and not from rampant curiosity about the earl, that she asked.

"Not lifelong, no. But he's a fine fellow, that one."

Was he? She watched how he smiled at Clarissa, and how her friend's cheeks flushed as bright as cherries. She was unaccountably irked—at him, for charming her friend, and at Clarissa, for succumbing to it. Even more annoying was how attractive he was while doing it. Some gentlemen were beginning to wear their hair unpowdered, but no one else did it with such brazenness. His hair was as black as coal, with long loose waves any woman would weep to have. In a room of snowy white coiffures, he caught the eye and held it—her eye, at any rate. It didn't hurt that he was tall and broadshouldered as well, standing above all the ladies and most of the men. She savagely hoped he did step on Clarissa's toe, quite heavily, and then wondered at herself for wishing such hurt on her friend.

When the minuet finished, Lord Dowling escorted Clarissa to them. "Eccleston, I'm in your debt."

Mr. Eccleston laughed. "As long as you brought her back to me, Dowling! Well, well, Clarissa, have you decided to abandon me for this rogue?"

Clarissa smiled. Her eyes sparkled and her cheeks were almost glowing. "Don't be silly! We all know Lord Dowling has other interests. But oh my heavens, sir, you are the most divine dancer! I have never felt so light on my feet. It was . . . oh, my . . . quite a pleasure!" She groped for her fan and plied it vigorously.

"I would not be satisfied with anything less than your pleasure," said Dowling with one of his sinful smiles.

"Hmph," said Mr. Eccleston, although without any real anger. Margaret was amazed and a little indignant over his careless attitude. "You'd better dance with me now, so I don't get a fit of jealousy."

"Oh, Freddie." Clarissa made a face at him, but Margaret could see she was enormously pleased. Clarissa Stacpoole had probably never in her life had two gentlemen wanting to dance with her and tease her.

"Very nicely done, sir," she said to Lord Dowling as Mr. Eccleston led Clarissa to join the dancers.

"Was it?" He flashed her a small smile. Standing right beside her, hands clasped behind his back, he was nearly overwhelming. "She's very light on her feet. Very accomplished in the minuet."

"Yes," said Margaret with some surprise. "She is." And Clarissa loved to dance. When Mr. Eccleston wasn't in attendance, she sighed more than once over the fact that no one else would ask her to step out. Perhaps it was a kind thing Lord Dowling had done after all. "I hope you haven't stirred up trouble by asking her."

"Nonsense," he said with a grin. "Eccleston has nothing to fear from me; he's exceptionally fond of her, and from her conversation, I gather she feels the same for him. I wouldn't dream of dividing them." He paused and gave her a sideways look. "They belong together, you know."

Precisely what he'd said to her about the pair of them. She narrowed her eyes in suspicion. "And you are qualified to sit in judgment, deciding who must marry whom?"

"You give me too much credit. Perhaps it's more divine than that; perhaps God himself designed the one to suit the other, and it would be a violation of natural law for them to be parted." He inclined his head, clearly enjoying himself greatly. "I merely have the discernment to see it."

"You must be one of the few," she said dryly. "I can see no fewer than a dozen violations of natural law in this very room, if suitability of marriage partners qualifies as a sin."

"It is such a shame when fathers and brothers ignore God's

will." He lowered his voice. "How fortunate you are, to have secured your own choice in the matter."

"Is this part of your plan to coerce me into marriage?"

He tilted his head, looking at her, and then turned to face her fully. "No, Miss de Lacey. I would never attempt coercion. I'm content to wait until you see how right we are for each other."

She waited, but he said nothing else, to her annoyance. Then she was annoyed with herself, for realizing she had been waiting all this time in expectation of an invitation to dance, and that she would have accepted it, no matter how impertinent he was. Part of her, like Clarissa, yearned to dance with such a man. "Are you not even going to ask me to dance, then?" she asked, striving for lightness. "For if not, I beg you go away. Your presence is keeping all the other gentlemen at bay."

"And are you sorry for that?" His eyes glittered with sly amusement.

"If it means I shan't get to dance, yes," she said, lying very boldly.

"I see." He made a very elegant bow, giving her a good look at his well-shaped leg. "I bid you good evening then, since I wouldn't dream of denying you any pleasure." And he turned and walked away, leaving her gaping in astonishment at his back.

And so it went for more than a fortnight. She saw him everywhere, and he made a point of speaking to her each time. He was amusing, insightful, and thoughtful, much more so than she would have expected. Before long she began looking for him—she suspected Clarissa was letting him know, through Mr. Eccleston, which events she planned to attend—and she never again made the mistake of telling him to go away. But he never asked her to dance, or to stroll with him in the garden, or even if he might call on her. It was maddening. Everyone, from Miss Cuthbert to Mr. Eccleston, was certain he was planning to propose to her. But aside from some offhand references to pleasing her, he never said anything even remotely connected to marriage or love.

Finally she could bear it no more. One evening at Vauxhall, where he joined her in the elegant supper box Francis had taken, she turned to him and asked bluntly, "Are you courting me?"

His eyebrows went up, but she would swear he was pleased. "Miss de Lacey," he said softly. "How forward you are."

"Don't tell me you're surprised to discover it now."

He smiled at her dry tone. "I never said I was surprised. In fact . . ." He shifted in his chair, maneuvering closer so he could stroke one fingertip over the back of her hand, lying folded in her lap. "It is one of the many things I like about you."

"You would, impertinent rogue." But she couldn't help smiling.

"Shh," he murmured. "Miss Cuthbert will send me away if you appear to enjoy my impertinent ways."

She bit the inside of her cheek to keep from laughing. Miss Cuthbert had slowly warmed to him; now her warnings that Lord Dowling was ineligible sounded rote and dutiful instead of worried or even sincere, and she had stopped fretting and frowning every time he spoke to her. Dowling had the knack of charming women with simple decency, Margaret thought. Clarissa, whom he danced with regularly, was fully converted. So far from whispering in horrified fascination about his Welsh wildness, now she rhapsodized about his grace, his thoughtfulness, and his dark good looks, which were, in her opinion, too appealing by half, especially when coupled with that faint Welsh accent. Margaret had given up trying to disagree.

"I think you are avoiding my question, sir."

He looked at her a moment. Francis had abandoned them as soon as he showed their silver admission token at the gates, Miss Cuthbert had excused herself a few moments earlier, and Clarissa had pulled Mr. Eccleston into the opposite corner, where they sat very close together in deep conversation. She and Lord Dowling might almost have been alone, as long as they kept their voices low. "Would you like me to court you?" the earl finally asked.

Yes. She smoothed her hands over her skirts to keep from confessing it aloud. "I would like to know if you are," she replied. "Or what your intentions are, if you aren't."

"My intentions . . ." His slow smile acted like a torch held to her skin. She felt prickly with heat and yet transfixed by the glowing allure of it. "I intend to have you, Maggie, in every way a man can have a woman. I want your hand in mine while we dance. I want you laughing beside me in the theater. I want you lying naked in my arms at night. And I want you standing beside me in church, saying 'I will.'" His gaze scorched her. "What are *your* intentions?"

Margaret's mouth was bone dry. She couldn't have answered if she'd known what to say. She wanted all that, too—she even wanted it from him—and if he wanted her dowry, too, well, why shouldn't Francis's money be appreciated? It wasn't as though her other suitors didn't want it.

She wet her lips and forced her throat to work. "Come with me." She got to her feet and moved toward the door, shooting a look at Clarissa when her friend glanced up in surprise. Clarissa's eyes darted to Dowling, on his feet and following close behind her, and she gave Margaret a tiny smile brimming with glee.

Outside the box, Lord Dowling offered his arm, and she laid her hand on it very properly. They strolled along the gravel walk, well lit by a profusion of oil lamps hung among the branches of the trees. Behind them the orchestra played, and the murmurs of conversation from other supper boxes didn't quite drown out the singer. Margaret took a deep breath and sighed with pleasure at the sight. She had always liked Vauxhall, even though Miss Cuthbert sniffed at its lack of exclusivity. Her parents had brought her to Vauxhall during her long-ago debut, and those trips figured among her happiest memories of that time. Ranelagh was more fashionable, but there was something a bit easier and less restrained about Vauxhall, where the lowest maid in London could walk out with her beau and make as merry as any heiress.

The path grew dimmer, the lamps less numerous as they moved through the Grove. Dowling seemed content to let her lead, and she searched carefully for the right spot. She took care not to wander too far from the path, mindful of being pursued by Miss Cuthbert, but wanted some privacy for what she had to ask of him.

Finally they reached a darkened turn of the path. This far from the orchestra and main walks, the cooing of thrushes and a pair of nightingales murmured around them. She stopped and faced Lord Dowling, suddenly nervous but trying to hide it. They had spent a great deal of time together, but never truly alone. "If you intend to marry me," she said, "you'd better kiss me first."

His gaze dropped to her mouth. "Now?" he murmured in his dark, raspy voice.

"Yes." She swallowed. "Please do."

He continued to look at her mouth. "You haven't answered my question yet, about your intentions. I hope you don't plan to tease me and seduce me, only to refuse me later, madam."

The notion of her seducing him was so—so—*tempting*—no, not tempting, *ridiculous*— She took an unsteady breath. "You claim we suit each other. Prove it."

Rhys took a step closer. Prove it. He longed to prove it to her, to kiss her until she moaned in his arms, to carry her deeper into the woods and show her just how much he wanted her and how well he could satisfy all her longings. His blood was coursing hot and fast in anticipation, but he kept a tight leash on his visceral reaction to her bold demand. "Is this the last question in your mind? Your last doubt?"

Her expressive lips parted. The silver pendant on her choker winked at him, fluttering ever-so-slightly on the rapid throb of her pulse. "No, not quite the very last," she said. "But it is an important one."

Dimly he supposed the last one was still about the money, that damned dowry that cast every suitor in a shady, avaricious light. Courtesy of Miss Stacpoole's wagging tongue, he knew three other men had already proposed marriage to Margaret, and she had turned them all down. Two were acknowledged fortune hunters, but one was a decent fellow with expectations. He had steadfastly resisted the urge to ask her about other suitors, but that third refusal gave him hope. He could tell she liked his attentions. His strategy of charming her friends had done wonders to thaw her opinion of him. He even found he liked Miss Stacpoole and her Freddie, which was fortunate; it seemed clear they would be part of his life for as long as Margaret was.

But best of all was that the lady herself only improved on closer acquaintance. The sharp tongue and undaunted spirit that flayed him so mercilessly when they first met were scintillating, when not turned on him. Even when she did turn on him a little, he still found it more exhilarating than shrewish. One evening they had a vigorous disagreement over the American colonies, where his fortune had gone to wither in the hot Carolina sun. Rhys was all in favor of letting those benighted lands go and good riddance, while she strongly felt such a valuable possession should be retained if at all possible. Arguing with an intelligent, informed woman was a novel experience for him; she acknowledged his points, but had sound points of her own. When she made him admit he would support sending British troops to protect private British property and investments, despite his disgust for anything to do with the Americas, he knew he was hers. Wanting a woman was one thing. Finding her fascinating was another.

Now he stared down at her upturned face, pale and unearthly in the moonlight. Kiss her, she asked. He'd dreamed of nothing else for weeks. He raised his hand to her jaw, letting his fingers brush over the exposed swells of her breasts, pushed high by her stomacher. She inhaled sharply at his touch, and he took advantage of the motion to draw her to him. Her waist felt small and slender under his hand, nipped in under her corset and the folds of her mulberry silk gown, but when her body pressed against his, it was unmistakably a woman's body.

He stroked her cheek, fingering a loose tendril of hair before smoothing it back. No one wore powder to Vauxhall, and her pale tresses were as soft as silk. "How many kisses?" he murmured.

"Just one will do." She sounded as breathless as he felt. Good. Raw male satisfaction ripped through him. He was no green boy, undone by the sight of a woman's parted lips, but by God, he wanted her to be as aroused by this as he was.

"How long a kiss?" He brushed his lips against the corner of her mouth.

"How long do you need?" She swayed against him, her hand resting lightly against his chest.

"To kiss you properly?" He smiled. "A lifetime, Maggie." And finally he kissed her.

Rhys had no expectation that it was her first kiss. She had alluded to a debut in her youth, and since her brother ascended to the dukedom, she must have had dozens of suitors. It certainly wasn't his first kiss, either, and he could see benefits to being the last man to kiss a woman instead of the first.

But it was *their* first kiss, and he wanted it to make an impression—and leave her aching for more.

Her lips were soft against his. For a moment he just savored the feel of them—and the feel of her, in his arms—but it wasn't enough. He deepened the kiss, sucking lightly at her lower lip until she gasped. Rhys pressed his advantage a little, tasting her mouth, sweet with arrack punch. He flattened one hand against the small of her waist, drawing her to him, and felt her fingers curl into the facings of his coat. Satisfaction fizzed in his veins. Kissing her was more delightful than expected, even if she was more pliant than responsive.

And then, Margaret gave a soft sigh before she went up on her toes and began kissing him back.

Rhys was not prepared for it. Of all the kisses in his life, none had ever been so honest and so longing. He could taste the desire in her, from the way her tongue twined with his to the way her body strained against his. She clung to him as if she would never let go, and the flare of lust shot right to his groin. Good Lord. He'd expected to be the seducer, and instead he was drowning in desire, so hard for her he could hardly stay on his feet. He cupped his shaking hand around the back of her skull, and threw restraint to the winds.

"I say there, sir," said a frosty voice behind them some minutes later. "Unhand the lady!"

Margaret gave a violent start in his arms. Rhys held her for a moment so she wouldn't fall, then loosened his grip and let her step away. She looked delectable; her hair had gotten a bit mussed, and her breasts were almost spilling from her bodice. Another sign how much he'd lost himself, that he had gone so far in a place where they could be interrupted at any moment. He turned to the intruder slowly, giving a discreet tug to right his breeches and blocking Margaret from sight so she could repair herself, only to grimace when he recognized the fellow. "Always taking an interest in other people's affairs, aren't you, Branwell?" he asked dryly.

The Marquis of Branwell drew himself up and glared back. "I might have known it would be you assaulting a lady in a public garden, Dowling." He craned his neck to the side. "Are you well, Miss de Lacey?"

"Yes, yes, perfectly well," she said breathlessly, stepping around Rhys. "What made you think otherwise, sir?"

Branwell's nostrils flared in obvious disgust as he glanced at Rhys. "Perhaps you are not aware, Miss de Lacey, that the paths in the Grove are not safe for the delicate sex. This part of the garden is frequented by scoundrels."

"So I have heard." She smiled regally, despite the blond curl drooping from her coiffure. "I shall be alert for any, sir. Thank you for the warning."

Branwell pointedly looked Rhys up and down. "You have already erred rather badly, madam, if your goal is to avoid scoundrels. I will escort you back to your brother, who will no doubt be appalled by your actions."

Rhys felt her slightly shocked glance, and wanted to punch Branwell in the face. How dare that priggish hypocrite poke his nose into the concerns of others? "No need, sir," he said thinly. "I'm escorting Miss de Lacey this evening."

The marquis physically recoiled. He shot Margaret a look of pure disdain before turning the same expression on Rhys. "So I see. I might have known you would try to remedy your problems by luring a woman into ruin. Your father would be ashamed."

Rhys curled his mouth in grim imitation of a smile, and swept an elaborate bow. Branwell hissed in disapproval. Without a word of farewell he turned on his heel and walked away.

The silence was ringing. All the heat and glow of the kiss had faded into nothing, like a fire put out by a bucket of cold water.

"Not a friend of yours, I presume," said Margaret softly after a minute.

"No," he muttered. "Rather the opposite."

Her skirts rustled as she came to stand beside him. "I hear such wicked things of you," she said. "Everyone except Clarissa assures me you're purely after my fortune and are such a rascal, my ears would burn to hear of it. And yet my own eyes tell me something different." She paused. "I'm sure I wouldn't have to beg a true scoundrel to kiss me."

He smiled without humor. "What do your eyes tell you about me? I confess I would like to know."

She studied him. "You dance with my friend, when other gentlemen laugh at her looks and snub her for her frankness. You are cordial to her fiancé, whom society mocks as a dim-witted fool. You bow out when I tease you that your company discourages other men from asking me to dance. You say you want to marry me, but then talk to me of politics and busi-ness, of family and home—of things that truly matter to me— rather than flirting and praising my fine eyes. And now a man insults you to your face, and you bow as if he did you great honor. I cannot understand it."

"No?" He sighed. "Perhaps it makes no sense."

"It makes sense," she said slowly, "if you are an exceedingly cagey fellow who will go to great lengths to fool me about the depths of your devotion. Or . . . if you really care to know me."

Rhys looked down at her. Her face, even turned up to his, was dim and shadowed in the faint moonlight, but he remem-bered the feel of her lips against his, of her cheek against his. He'd meant to tell her all this, but not tonight, when he wanted only to revel in the passion that sparkled between them. His courtship had gone almost perfectly, from the discovery that they were well suited to each other in intellect, temperament, humor, and now physical desires. He was sure he could have proposed tonight and been accepted, if not for the yawning difference in their financial states and the aspersions it cast on his motives. Cursed Branwell.

"I dance with Miss Stacpoole because it gives her as much pleasure as it gives me. Eccleston is no scholar but he's a decent, honest man and a steadfast fellow. He doesn't care how I choose to address my financial straits." He paused, but there was no way to avoid it. The marquis would surely tell her brother, and this was his only chance to explain before others told Margaret Branwell's version of the tale. "Branwell was my guardian—my father's cousin who managed my estates until I reached my majority."

"He—what?" she exclaimed. "You said your guardian squandered the estate!"

"He doesn't see it that way." Rhys shrugged, trying to keep the familiar, well-worn ire at bay. "I notice he didn't make the same investments with his own funds, though. But he will never forgive me for revealing how low the Dowling fortunes had sunk when I came of age, casting well-earned blame for it on him."

"Revealing," she repeated. "How does one hide it? Especially a marked reduction in circumstances?"

She really was from a different society, if she didn't know. "By living on credit. By using your station and name to intimidate merchants into supplying you, while never paying their bills. By bleeding every farthing out of your lands and tenants in order to maintain appearances, while they starve. An earl must live like a nobleman, not like a vagabond, even if he is as poor as one," he finished a bit harshly, remembering Branwell's last lecture to him on the subject.

"A vagabond." Her voice rang with doubt, as if to say, how can a man who attends balls be a vagabond?

Suddenly he was just tired of it. Margaret knew he was destitute; he'd already admitted it to her himself, even though she'd heard it from a dozen other sources as well. After taking such care to get to know her, what was the point in hiding the truth now? If she couldn't stomach it, better that he know now. "I've sold everything I can," he said quietly. "The plate, the silver, the furnishings, the paintings, the rare books . . . everything my father collected and Branwell approved of. All that's left is entailed, but it's crumbling around my ears. I don't believe an earldom entitles a man to amass as much debt as he can and ignore the bills. But I've reached the end of what I can do. There is nothing left to sell, no more source of funds." He sighed again. "Damned foolish sheep."

"And that's why you need to marry an heiress," she whispered.

"Clyve persuaded me to that. After spending the last ten years trying to salvage my estate, and being beset by one disaster after another, I personally favored putting the whole property into Holland covers and decamping for the Continent. Perhaps try my luck at tending goats in the Alps." He gave her a wry look. "The very course you urged upon me when we met."

She didn't smile. "You really would have abandoned your estate?"

"It's damn near a ruin at this point. My father was so obsessed with collecting objets d'art, he let the house fall into extreme disrepair. The roof collapsed on one wing, the gardens were let go when my mother remarried, Branwell tried to cover his losses by letting servants go so there's been no one to keep out the weather . . . It's in such a state I cannot even lease it out." He shrugged. "I would sell it all if I could break the entail. The house in town at least is still whole."

"What will you do if . . . ?" Her voice trailed off uncomfortably.

"If I cannot seduce a wealthy lady into marriage?"

She bit her lip, looking about to cry. He repented his bitter remark. "There, darling," he murmured, pulling her into his arms. She laid her cheek on his shoulder, and he took a deep breath. God. If only he'd had as much money as she did, or even just a little bit. Then she wouldn't doubt him. "I thank God for your brother's generosity," he whispered. "I might not have met you but for the gossip about your dowry—along with Clyve's mother, of course, who put your name on a list of potential brides for him."

"For Lord Clyveden?" She sounded appalled, and Rhys smiled.

"He gave me the list and persuaded me to meet the ladies on it. Your name was the third of four."

"Who else was on the list?"

He made a dismissive sound. "Mere girls. One meek and quiet, one amiable and ambitious."

"That's only two."

"I never even met the fourth, Maggie," he breathed against her temple. "Once I met you, and you gave me such a magnificent set-down, I knew you were the only woman for me."

He could feel her cheek swell with a little smile, but then

she stepped back and regarded him soberly. "But if I didn't have a dowry, you wouldn't be here with me in this garden, would you?" In the moonlight she was beautiful, her eyes dark and serious, her skin glowing like pearl.

"I think I would be," he said. "If you were still that spinster in Holborn without a pound to your name, and I had met you some other way, I would still be here, hoping to kiss you again."

"If I were still a spinster in Holborn," she said slowly, "everyone would mock you for even looking twice at me."

"My darling Maggie," he said with a faint smile, "they've already turned their backs on me. I would live my life in ruin and disgrace for the chance to look twice at you, every day for the rest of eternity."

Her breathing stopped. "Why?" she asked, almost fearfully.

If he hadn't already declared himself with his last statement, there was no reason not to come straight out and say it. He met her eyes and said simply, "Because I'm falling in love with you."

CHAPTER SEVEN

Rhys went home not knowing if he had lost his chance with Margaret. Part of him feared very much he had; her reaction to his declaration of love had been underwhelming. She turned away as if flustered or unsettled, and only nodded when he offered to take her back to her party. They had parted with subdued, empty niceties, and Rhys left with no idea if his feelings upset her or pleased her.

Until Branwell's untimely arrival, he'd thought very differently. She wanted to know his intentions, and if he were courting her. She asked him to walk out, and told him to kiss her—it was important to her, knowing if they suited each other physically. And by God, did she suit him. She suited him so well, he was awake until the small hours of the morning, reliving the feel of her mouth on his, her body pressed against his, her rapid breath against his cheek as he kissed every inch of her lovely throat.

But now his secrets were out. Although everyone in London knew he was destitute, he hadn't exactly flaunted the depth of his fall. He was righteously proud he had stopped the mindless borrowing against his lands begun by his father and continued with abandon under Branwell's hand despite his protests, but that pride had a sour taste. Perhaps he should have kept up the pretense a little longer, at least until he secured a wealthy bride, when he could have discreetly turned his fortunes around. Not that he would have lied to Margaret, precisely, but he wouldn't have had to tell her until he was more certain of her feelings for him.

He was ruminating over it when Clyve arrived, bearing a leg of ham and the morning papers. "You need to marry the girl quickly, so you can provide a decent breakfast for your friends," he told Rhys, sending the ham off with Bunter, the one remaining servant, for carving.

"I've no idea if she'll marry me at all. Cousin Branwell turned up in the garden last night at a very inopportune moment."

Clyve groaned. "That idiot! But surely all isn't lost—you said she's a sensible woman. Anyone with sense can see Branwell's a narrow-minded fool."

"She is," said Rhys dourly. "No doubt she'll make the sensible decision and refuse me."

His friend waved one hand. "What sort of inopportune moment?"

"*Very* inopportune."

"Excellent," cried Clyve with a leer. "Good work, Dowling. To your upcoming marriage." He lifted his cup of coffee in salute.

"No, no." Rhys glared at him. "Of course I didn't make love to her in the gardens at Vauxhall. Be sensible, Clyve."

"If Branwell starts telling everyone you did, it's as good as done." Clyve shrugged, unconcerned.

"The old fool better keep his mouth closed," said Rhys sharply. "If he doesn't, I'll close it for him."

The viscount looked mildly surprised. "Isn't that what you want? If Branwell tells people you've had her, her brother will have little choice but to give his consent."

He didn't answer. Clyve only saw the goal and a means to achieve it. Rhys, though, hated the thought of Margaret being forced to marry him. Not only would it counter all the efforts he'd made to prove his interest in her, not her dowry, it would infuriate her, even if she didn't believe him guilty of engineering that scene in Vauxhall. Was it too much to ask of fate that this one point of desire in his life, this small question of personal happiness, not go spectacularly wrong?

"Come now," Clyve relented when he was silent. "It ain't so bad as that! I know you liked her best, but buck up, man— there are other heiresses in London. If Durham spurns your offer, take another turn at the Cranmore girl. I hear she refused Simington the other day because he was a mere baron."

"Who?" Rhys frowned and waved Clyve's answer aside. "No."

His friend sat back and looked at him in surprise. "You're smitten," he declared, half amused, half disgusted. "By the saints, how did you let that happen?"

Rhys didn't bother replying. Bunter brought in the ham, neatly sliced, and set it on the table, along with a fresh pot of coffee, before disappearing out the door again.

Clyve speared a slice of ham from the platter and rolled it up. "What you need to do, then, is secure the lady's affections." He took a bite of his ham and chewed, looking thoughtful. "I gather that's the only obstacle."

"Yes, that was my plan," he said dryly.

"She went off into the shrubbery with you, so she's not indifferent."

"No." Not at all, from the way she kissed him back. He inhaled deeply at the memory. Another few kisses like that. . .

"You need to have her alone, then," Clyve went on. "Exert some persuasion."

Another few kisses like that . . . would tell him what he needed to know. If she didn't care for him, for whatever reason, he would know to move on. If she did, though . . . Margaret was no meek, limp creature. He remembered the way she had put him in his place in Chelsea, and a smile touched his lips for the first time all day. "Clyve, I do believe you're right."

"Of course I am." Clyve folded the rest of his ham into his mouth and wiped his hands on the tablecloth.

The knocker on the front door sounded, echoing through the hall. Rhys heard Bunter rush to answer it, and a moment later Freddie Eccleston appeared in the doorway, a pair of dogs at his heels. "Morning, Dowling," he said cheerfully. "Clyveden."

Brilliant. Eccleston had taken to stopping by whenever he had a message regarding Margaret. Rhys had never asked him to do it; he suspected Miss Stacpoole told him to all on her own. Like Clyve, she seemed to think Rhys needed every aid in winning Margaret's heart. Rhys was growing exceptionally fond of Miss Stacpoole. "Come in. Have some breakfast." He waved one hand at the table, even though it only held the ham and coffee.

Eccleston took a seat, his dogs creeping under the chair at his command. "I have information for you," he said directly, taking a slice of ham and tearing it into shreds. "You're to attend the masque at Carlisle House three evenings hence." The two dogs' noses emerged from under his chair, and Eccleston fed a piece of ham to each twitching snout. "You must wear dark colors and a domino, and I was assured it would not go amiss if you were to wear a hat with a large, dashing plume in it as well."

Clyve gave a bark of laughter. Rhys grinned, but in growing jubilation instead of amusement. "What else does Miss Stacpoole recommend?"

"You should look for a lady wearing white and black, with a garland of flowers on her head." Eccleston paused. "I endured quite a description of how striking it will be, so take careful notice, Dowling."

"Good God," drawled Clyve, lounging in his chair with an air of wicked delight. "I haven't been to a masque in some time. I might have such a hat at home . . ."

"Excellent; I'd be delighted to borrow it. Bunter will fetch it at once," Rhys told him. "What time should I seek the lady in white and black?"

"Not before ten o'clock." Eccleston fed more scraps of ham to the patient dogs before pinning a serious look on Rhys. "I also am to advise you that the Duke of Durham does not care for masquerades, and will not be in attendance, fortunately for you."

"Bugger him," scoffed Clyve, but Rhys waved him into silence.

"He disapproves?"

"He was vehemently displeased by your wandering about Vauxhall the other night." Done distributing the ham, Eccleston put his hand under the chair, where it was lovingly washed by his hounds. "He gave me quite a glare when Miss de Lacey returned to the supper box looking pale and flustered, even though she told him she was quite well and he needn't worry. Sent us right out, with the companion, too. Clarissa said they argued when they reached home, but she regards Miss de Lacey as a sort of queenly tiger, and quite capable of holding her own." Rhys grinned at the description. "Still, His Grace won't be pleased to see you, no matter what his sister says. Not much gentlemanly decorum in that one."

"Not a gentleman at all," sniffed Clyve.

"I think he'd cut out your liver with his own knife, if you crossed him," added Eccleston.

"He promised her she would have her choice," Rhys said, beginning to hum with elated anticipation. "And it appears she is on the brink of making it."

CHAPTER EIGHT

If Margaret had any illusions about her brother's attention or temper altering under the weight of his ducal crown, she was swiftly disabused.

She took her time going back into the box in Vauxhall, still trying to sort out her feelings over what had happened on her walk with Lord Dowling. First, and most delightfully, he kissed her—and so spectacularly well, her knees still felt a bit weak. She could see fewer and fewer reasons not to encourage his suit: He was charming, attentive, thoughtful, decent, and bloody beautiful, as Clarissa so aptly put it. He held her as if he could hardly restrain his baser urges, and his kiss . . . She touched unsteady fingers to her lips, remembering. Would he really have kissed her that way when she was still a spinster from Holborn? Would he have said to her then, as he did tonight, that he was losing his heart to her? Margaret was becoming more and more certain he might have. And the less she believed him to be just another bankrupt in search of a rich wife, the more she admitted she might be falling in love, too.

Fortunately she sent him off before walking into what

turned out to be a bitter quarrel. Francis, who had hitherto shown a commendable lack of interest in her suitors, was waiting when she returned. She knew it would be bad when she found him alone in the supper box. Instinctively she halted in the doorway.

"Where were you?" he asked through thin lips, his arms folded over his chest.

"Walking. Where were you?" She looked around the box. "Where have Clarissa and Mr. Eccleston gone? And Miss Cuthbert?"

"Eccleston took Miss Stacpoole home, with Miss Cuthbert chaperoning. Where were you?" he repeated.

"I went for a stroll with Lord Dowling." There was no reason to lie, as everyone had seen them leave.

"Dowling," he said harshly. "Dowling, the Welsh earl who hasn't a shilling to his name?"

"Dowling, the charming gentleman who's become my friend?" She widened her eyes. "Yes, that's the one."

"The one who's after your dowry, you mean."

"Pish." Margaret laughed lightly, sensing his temper was truly engaged and trying to divert it. "That bloody dowry. You really ought to take it back, Francis."

"That's what he wants, Meg," her brother warned, ignoring her attempts. "Don't allow yourself to be seduced by a wastrel."

"How do you know he's a wastrel?" she demanded, irked. "How do you know he's any different from Lord Sandridge or Viscount Lavoy?"

He glowered at her. "I've heard tales."

"Tales of what? Dead sheep?" She shook her head. "How is his misfortune any different than Mr. Twiston's?" The Twistons had been their neighbors in Holborn. Francis had been compassionate and generous in helping them when they went bankrupt after Mr. Twiston's shop and everything in it burned to the ground. Surely he must remember that part of himself.

"Tales of willful negligence of his estates. Tales of his flagrant disregard for his tenants and dependents. Tales of shocking financial neglect."

"Lord Branwell told you that, didn't he?" She pursed her lips. "Did he mention he was Lord Dowling's guardian after the death of his father, and many of the debts and bad investments were made on his orders?"

His face darkened, and he didn't argue. Margaret savored the hit. "I don't like him."

"Like him?" she exclaimed in astonishment. "You've never met him!"

"I know he's in desperate want of funds, and I know he led you off into the dark Grove alone. I shall speak to Miss Cuthbert about that."

"Really, Francis," she snapped without thinking. "I'm a woman of thirty, not some silly girl of sixteen. I invited him to walk with me, and Miss Cuthbert had nothing to do with it." He stared at her, his eyes glittering in the glow of the oil lamps. "I was perfectly fine," she added. "He did nothing I didn't wish him to do."

"I see." He jerked his head. "We're going home."

"Very well."

"And you're not to see him again."

Margaret flushed with outrage and fury from head to toe. "Not see him again?" she repeated. "How *dare* you. You promised me I would have my choice of suitors."

"Subject to my approval," he growled.

"You never said that! My choice, you declared," she said savagely. "*Mine*. Dowling is no more a wastrel than you are, Francis. Have the decency to meet the man before you judge him so harshly."

"I'll judge him as I wish." He tossed her cloak at her. "Come."

"Are you a man of your word or not?" She clutched the cloak but made no effort to put it on.

"I gave my word," he said. "To our father. I promised I'd protect you, and I intend to."

She narrowed her eyes at him. "Then don't be an idiot about it." She swirled the cloak about her shoulders and left, ignoring him as he strode next to her to the dock, boarded the wherry, and crossed the river. Not a word was spoken in the carriage on the way back to Berkley Square, and he went straight to his study while she stormed upstairs.

But once there her heart began to tighten with anxiety instead of anger. If Francis forbade her to see Dowling again, what would she do? None of her other suitors engaged her interest half as much as he did. Lord Weston was a decent fellow, and Lord Camersley was pleasant enough and very handsome, but none of them had Lord Dowling's blend of irreverent humor and kindness and wicked smiles. None of the others made her think they wanted her, naked in their arms at night, as Lord Dowling did. Margaret was not an innocent girl to be shocked by such talk. She had seen love and passion, good marriages and bad, and she knew what she wanted for herself.

The next morning she was on the brink of sending Clarissa

a note when the lady herself appeared, wide-eyed and burning with curiosity.

"Are you well?" she demanded even before her bonnet was off. "Oh, Margaret, I was so worried last night—Freddie was so grim when His Grace sent us home, and Miss Cuthbert was almost in tears!"

"Come into my sitting room," Margaret said, mindful of the servants. "Miss Cuthbert should be waiting." She led the way to the stairs to her suite of rooms, and firmly closed the door. "I need your help," she told her two potential accomplices.

Miss Cuthbert paled. She already looked wretched, and had been on the verge of tears all morning. "Miss de Lacey, I am mortified at what my actions have exposed you to."

"What happened last night?" cried Clarissa. "Did Dowling—?"

"No." Margaret pulled a chair closer and lowered her voice. "Lord Dowling did nothing wrong. In fact, he did everything right. I—I believe I am in great danger of being hopelessly in love with him."

"Oh, Miss de Lacey," began Miss Cuthbert in a wobbly voice.

"Brilliant," exclaimed Clarissa, beaming. "I knew it! He could not be so charming and so bloody beautiful and not win your heart! Freddie will be so pleased to hear it, he regards Dowling as a great friend—we shall be like sisters!"

Margaret held up her hand, not smiling. "It isn't as simple as that. If you haven't already heard, you soon will. Lord Branwell, who was Dowling's guardian when his father died, is telling terrible stories impugning Dowling's decency and intelligence. He told my brother last evening Dowling is only after my fortune, and now Durham says he forbids me to see Dowling again."

Clarissa's mouth opened, and closed. "Oh dear," she whispered.

"But you wish to see the gentleman again." Miss Cuthbert sounded wistful. "You favor him."

Margaret gave a tiny nod. "I do." She had been awake all night, sorting through her feelings and the facts of her situation. "Yes, I favor him. Greatly." Clarissa wiggled in her chair, beaming again. "Miss Cuthbert, I know you advised me he is unsuitable—"

"Nonsense," said her companion quietly. "I was hasty. He's not as eligible as some, it is true . . . But he is an earl of good character. I have never heard him called rude or debauched. Most of his troubles stem from his dire financial circumstances, which he hasn't lied about or hidden, as some of our class do. I—I believe you might do far worse, Miss de Lacey."

"She could hardly do better," put in Clarissa as Margaret stared at her companion in surprise. "Dowling has a lovely estate. His father was a bit of an eccentric, always collecting books and paintings, his mother took herself off as soon as he was cold in his grave, and then Dowling was left to the idiotic care of that Branwell, who is, you must admit, one of the silliest and stupidest of men."

"He is," Miss Cuthbert confirmed.

"My mother says it's a miracle Dowling is half as decent as he is. She's had her ear out for anything about him, now he and Freddie are inseparable. That Viscount Clyveden is a scoundrel, but even he is kind to his mother, which says so much about a man, I think."

"It does," Miss Cuthbert agreed. "And Dowling has been so gentlemanly toward Miss de Lacey."

Clarissa nodded. "No man could be better! Margaret, you are quite right to favor him, and I will do everything in my power to help you if you wish to run away with him."

"As will I," declared Miss Cuthbert, bright spots of color in her cheeks.

"Excellent." Margaret clasped her hands together in relief. "I knew I could depend on you both, although I don't wish to plan an elopement just yet. I merely want to see Lord Dowling again, alone if possible, to make everything clear between us. And it would be best if I can manage it without my brother knowing."

Miss Cuthbert and Clarissa proved themselves born conspirators. It took the three of them half an hour to settle on a suitable façade: a masquerade ball at Carlisle House in a few days' time, with notice of her costume sent ahead to Dowling so he might find her; and an alternative plan, should Francis grow suspicious and decide to accompany her to the masquerade despite his dislike of them. Clarissa would have Mr. Eccleston hire a carriage to wait outside, so Margaret and Dowling could slip away if desired. Clarissa eagerly volunteered to tell any necessary lies to cover Margaret's disappearance.

"Oh, what a caper!" She giggled. "All in the pursuit of true love. I vow, Freddie will be so charmed when he hears of it."

"As long as he understands, and conveys to Lord Dowling, the importance of secrecy," Miss Cuthbert told her sternly. "You mustn't say a word to *anyone* else, Miss Stacpoole."

Clarissa made a face. "Of course I wouldn't! And neither will Freddie. But oh—Margaret, we must see to your dress! It must be striking, and you must look beautiful!"

"Yes." Margaret smiled, her heart beginning to leap. She would see him again. She felt no compunction flouting Francis's command that she not see Dowling. Francis had given her his word, and then broken it the moment he didn't like her decision. She felt fully absolved of any guilt and was even sure her father would have agreed with her. Francis's head had gotten too big since his inheritance.

But she had to see Dowling again. Her heart had already decided he was the one, and her body still hummed from his embrace. She needed just one more conversation to make sure there were no more obstacles, but deep inside she suspected he was the man for her.

The plan succeeded marvelously. Miss Cuthbert had a hidden genius for subterfuge, even after enduring a blistering lecture from Francis for allowing Margaret out of her sight at Vauxhall. She stoically listened, made her profuse apologies, and returned to Margaret's suite to continue plotting.

For her costume Margaret took a simple white polonaise gown and stitched glossy black ribbons to it. Paired with a flounced petticoat, it was unbearably elegant. She liked the stark simplicity, although Clarissa fretted over it and finally persuaded her to add a garland of pink roses in her hair.

When the night arrived, she was waiting in the hall for the carriage to come around when her brother finally appeared. They hadn't met since that stone-silent ride home from Vauxhall, and for a moment it seemed as though time had paused since then as they regarded each other.

"You look striking," Francis said at last. He was haggard in the lamp light. "A masquerade?"

"Yes. One of Mrs. Cornelys's entertainments at Carlisle House."

He grunted. "Foolishness."

"Entertainment," she countered calmly, raising her jeweled half mask. "For pleasure."

Francis's gaze moved past her. "With decorum, of course." From the corner of her eye Margaret saw Miss Cuthbert sink into a curtsey, murmuring agreement. What a sly minx Miss Cuthbert was.

The footman opened the door as the coach pulled up to the steps. "Good night, Francis," Margaret said, moving toward the door without another glance at her brother.

"Enjoy yourself," he said gruffly.

She planned to. Her brother's quiet demeanor gave her a small pang; perhaps she should have stayed to see if he wished to patch up things between them. But he'd had three days to do so, and he hadn't made an effort to see her in that time, even though she'd been about the house every day. Her pride was quite as strong as his, and she settled into the coach seat without much regret.

The masque was in full swing when they arrived. Carlisle House was so crowded one could hardly walk through the rooms, let alone dance, but Margaret had no thought of anything but finding the earl. She made her way through the rooms as best she could, keeping her eyes open for Dowling, or even Clarissa. Mr. Eccleston had reported Lord Dowling received her message with gratitude and sent assurance he would be at Carlisle House, but Margaret began to realize they might both be present, both search for each other, and still never meet. All of London seemed to be packed into this one house, however grand and spacious it might be under normal circumstances. She barely even noticed the rooms, famous for their magnificent decoration, for the crush of men in velvet coats, women with towering hairstyles, a wild profusion of feathers and plumes everywhere, and the mingled miasma of too many colognes, perfumes, and body odors.

On the stairs she stopped, suddenly desperate to be outside. She tried to go forward, but was blocked. She looked behind her for Miss Cuthbert, but her companion was gone, lost in the crowd. Margaret fanned herself, unbearably hot and feeling as though she were being squeezed from all sides.

"My very dear Miss de Lacey." A gentleman doffed his oversized hat and made a shallow bow in front of her. "May I assist you? You look in need of some fresh air."

She gasped in relief as Lord Dowling's eyes twinkled at her. "Thank you, sir, please." She grabbed his arm and followed close behind him as he plowed straight through the throngs, not stopping until he pushed open a door and they were outside.

"Are you well?" His arm was around her, supporting her, as she filled her lungs with clean, cool air.

Finally she managed to smile at him. "Very well, now you're here."

There was a pause as he just looked at her, desire and concern mingled in his eyes. "I heard you encountered some difficulties after our last tête-à-tête."

"None I regard." A trio of gentlemen in masks burst from the door behind them, laughing loudly. Dowling stepped in front of her, making a show of replacing his hat in such a way that screened her face from their view. She gave him a coy smile. "A very handsome hat, sir."

"Isn't it?" He grinned, cocking his hat to set the long plume swaying. "Stole it from Clyve. He claimed it belonged to some Roundhead ancestor of his, but I think he bought it himself."

"You must keep it," she said. "I quite like it. You look very dashing."

"Then he shall never have it back," he replied with a wink. "I would go to any lengths to look dashing in your eyes."

Margaret blushed. "Will you walk with me again, sir?"

"To the ends of the earth, madam, to say nothing of back and forth in this garden." He led her away from the house. There was only a thin strip of land on this side of the house, and the smell of the nearby stables rose around them.

"I've been thinking of what you said the other night," she began, "and of what Lord Branwell charged. I wondered . . ."

"Yes?" he prompted when she fell silent.

"What would you do with the money?" she asked softly. "If you had it."

"Ah, yes," he murmured. "Worried I would spend it all on dashing hats? I assure you, my dear, I'm not so fashionable as that. I would use it to repair my house, pay my handful of foolishly loyal servants, and do my best to leave an estate worthy for my son to inherit."

Margaret drew a fortifying breath. "What if you never had a son? What if the woman you married was too old to have children at all?"

He thought for a second. "I would make the house fit for my bride, pay the servants, and settle down to a happy life with her alone. Perhaps I could experiment with sheep breeding, and raise Britain's first buoyant sheep."

She choked back a laugh. "You would be famous for generations to come."

He grinned, looking rather like a pirate with the absurd hat.

"Is your house really falling down?" she asked.

His smile faded. "Yes. The manor house had to be closed up after a fire. The town house needs some work as well." He hesitated. "Would you like to see it?"

She started. "Tonight?"

He nodded, his gaze never wavering from hers.

Margaret took a deep breath. She had been prepared to steal away on a carriage ride with him if necessary; what was the difference, if they stopped at a house on that ride? She looked up at his face. No trace of that slashing dimple was visible in his lean cheek, and his skin was dark in the moonlight. The hat brim shadowed his eyes so all she could see was the reflection of the light from the windows of Carlisle House. She had engineered this meeting tonight to decide once and for all if she wanted to marry him, if logic and sense would support what her heart, body, and soul craved. Surely it was logical to see how badly he needed her money.

Heart pounding, she nodded once. "Yes, Lord Dowling. I would."

CHAPTER NINE

The drive took more time than Margaret expected. Most fashionable society had moved west from the heart of the city to elegant new arrangements such as Berkeley Square, where Durham House stood. She could tell they weren't going that way, though, and finally she just asked.

"Er . . . yes," said Dowling ruefully. "My father wanted a grand showplace, but the only suitable property he could find was in Paddington. He had plans to found a great museum to house his collection, and designed the house accordingly. It's practically a country manor."

Margaret had been to fine houses in London, some of which included a great deal of open space. "I see." But she didn't, not really, until the hired carriage stopped in front of a grand building that looked more temple than home, quite isolated.

"It's very impressive," she said when he helped her down.

"Isn't it?" Lord Dowling shook his head. "Wait until you see the interior." He led her up the shallow steps to the enormous front door, and to her surprise took a key from his coat pocket. Servants were always standing by to open the door at Durham

House, and even in Holborn they'd had someone responsible for that. But Dowling let them in, closing the door behind her with a quiet boom that echoed through the empty house.

If he hadn't said he lived here, she would have thought it was deserted. Wide double doors stood open to her left into a high-ceilinged room that contained not a stick of furniture or a single object on the walls. The hall they stood in was similarly bare, with only a single candle shedding a dull light. The stairs at the side climbed into absolute darkness above. It was utterly silent.

"I didn't anticipate visitors." The earl took up the candle and lit a candelabrum on the mantle of the cold fireplace. As more light filled the hall, Margaret could make out the shabbiness of the room, from the scratched and scuffed floor to the cobwebs in the corners. Dowling looked around, his face grim. "Bunter, my man, goes off to bed early, and the cleaning is too much for one person. It's really not fit for ladies."

Margaret roused herself. "Nonsense. I'm not so henhearted as that. Is this the drawing room?"

He followed her into the cavernous room to the left. "I believe so. Nearly every room was designed more for the purpose of display, and less of living."

Her footsteps echoed in the dusty stillness. There were no draperies at the windows, and the light of the full moon lit the room. As her eyes adjusted, she could make out rectangles on the walls where paintings had been. "What happened to the collection?"

"Sold."

"Was it valuable?"

He hesitated. "Not as valuable as my father thought."

Meaning he had lost money selling it. Margaret walked on. "It's a lovely room," she offered.

"When the cupids aren't falling, I suppose."

"Cupids?" She stopped to look at him in bemusement.

He swept one arm through the air. "Hundreds of them. The plasterer must have been very fond of the little devils."

He was right. Margaret peered upward and saw dozens of fat-bellied cupids clinging to every foot of the elaborate cornice. It was too dark to see what they might have looked like, but in the moonlight streaming through the windows the effect was almost sinister. "How original," she said faintly.

"How damned ugly," Dowling countered.

She glanced at him, and burst out laughing. "Perhaps."

He was grinning. "They're hideous—you should see them in the bright light of day—and even worse, they're murderous. At least once a day there will be a smashing sound as one of them finally loses his grip on the wall and plummets to an ig-nominious end. I beg you stand away from the walls."

"Are they all over the house?" She could make out a few spots where cupids had obviously parted ways with the cornice.

"In every room," he said with resignation. "For uniformity, you see."

They strolled on through the dining room, the gallery, and the earl's study. The empty bookshelves had a forlorn look to them that tugged at Margaret's heart. Aside from a battered table with a mended leg and a few chairs in the dining room, there was no furniture at all, no draperies, no ornament of any kind. It was quite the loneliest thing she could imagine.

When they reached the hall again, Dowling turned to her. "Have you satisfied yourself? What else may I show you to put your mind at rest?"

Her heart skipped a beat. From the intent way he was looking at her, he meant more than the house's condition. "I certainly see how you could put funds to good use."

As if prompted, there was a crash from the room behind him. "Another cupid meets his doom," said Dowling. His expression didn't change. "But I wasn't referring to money."

Margaret was acutely aware of how alone they were. He could kiss her again, and no one would interrupt. He could sweep her into his arms and make love to her, and no one would stop him . . . including herself. "What do you mean, then, sir?"

"I told you weeks ago you were the woman for me." He began walking toward her, his steps ringing like a battering ram against her reserve. "I want you. I need you. And yes, your dowry will keep us in comfort. But I wouldn't want another woman with those funds. Only you, love." He touched a loose lock of her hair, curling it around his finger. "Say yes, Maggie darling," he whispered.

"You haven't even asked the question," she protested, swaying toward him.

"Marry me," he said against her lips.

"Yes," she said at once, and he kissed her.

Under the touch of his lips, her doubts fell aside. She was in his arms as much through her own volition as through his. She wanted to be here, alone, with him, damn the differences in their financial states. Her decision was made.

This time she licked his lips first. He smiled and let her deepen the kiss. He tasted of mint and something darker, richer. She ran her hands along his broad shoulders, and then daringly down his chest, awed and giddy with the feel of him. She marveled that he let her explore him so boldly, but little by little the balance was shifting. His palm slid around her waist, urging her against him. He touched her jaw, subtly tipping her head to a better angle. His tongue met hers softly, then more urgently.

The simmering heat of passion, so long denied in her life, roared into an inferno. She gripped his coat and clung to him, opening her mouth for his possession as she surrendered her body to his intoxicating touch. Up and down her back his hands traveled, molding her to him with devastating intimacy. The silent house around them was a cocoon of privacy and solitude, where any desires could be indulged and explored. She trembled with the force of those desires. An engagement was nearly legally wed. . .

"You inflame me," he whispered. His fingers shook as he smoothed them down the expanse of her bosom. "I should take you back to Carlisle House . . . Your companions will miss you . . ."

"I want to stay with you."

His dark eyes were fiery bright in the candles' glow. "In my bed?" he asked softly.

Margaret's heart leaped, tripped, and almost soared from her chest. "Yes."

He bowed his head, and one corner of his mouth curled upward. "I love you, Margaret de Lacey," he said, and then with one motion he caught her up in his arms. She looped one arm around his neck and crushed her frothy skirts with the other as he carried her up the stairs, down a short corridor, into a bedroom. There was a bit more furniture in this room, as well as a carpet, and the embers of a banked fire glowed in the grate when he set her back on her feet by the hearth and sank to his knees.

"Dowling," she began.

"Rhys." He looked up from stirring the fire. "My name is Rhys."

She blushed. "Will we be so informal? Miss Cuthbert assured me people of nobility never use Christian names."

"Miss Cuthbert also told you I was unsuitable, didn't she?" He gave her a sly grin. "Say it."

"Rhys." It suited him, a vaguely foreign name with an air of wildness about it. She said it again, letting it linger on her lips.

"It sounds like an invitation when you say it that way."

"Everything I've said has been an invitation tonight."

His eyebrows went up. He dropped the poker and rose to his feet. "Indeed! May I express my eternal gratitude to God and all the saints that you accepted me? There's not another woman like you in the world, Maggie."

She liked that nickname, better than Meg as her brother called her. Perhaps it sounded a bit more sensual and wicked in Rhys's faint accent as well. Regardless, she arched her neck and smiled. "And now?"

His expression sharpened on her. "Now, love, I intend to prove my devotion." He lifted Clarissa's garland of roses from her head and set it aside. "You've no more need of thorns with me."

She laughed. "Much deterrent they proved!"

He ran his fingertips lightly down her cheek, turning her face up to him. "For such a rare and beautiful bloom, I would brave a thousand thorns."

When he touched her and looked at her this way, she felt beautiful. No one else seemed to embrace her as she was. "Do you love me?" she whispered.

Rhys stilled. "I do."

Margaret smiled. "Then kiss me again."

He kissed her until her head swam. His nimble fingers unhooked her gown and lifted it over her head. Margaret gave up fumbling with the line of buttons that marched down his waistcoat, which prompted a low laugh from Rhys, and settled for untying her petticoat as he stripped off his garments. He made faster progress than she did, and she still wore her stockings and shift when he scooped her up and carried her to the bed.

"Thank goodness you kept some furniture," she said as he loomed over her, his knee between hers.

"The first thing I shall buy," he said between hot kisses along her neck, "is a grand new bed, fit for a countess."

She would be a countess, no longer Miss de Lacey but Lady Dowling. She hadn't even thought of that.

"And then," Rhys went on in a low growl, "I shall keep you in that bed for hours every day. Our servants will be outraged."

"Will they?" She could hardly speak from the thumping of her heart. Oh heavens, she had dreamed of this for so long, and never once imagined how desperate it would feel. How the slightest brush of his fingertips over the swell of her breast could make her skin sizzle. How his lips at the base of her throat could stoke some unknown urgency inside her. How she, sensible plain spinster Margaret Emily de Lacey, could curl her legs around his hips to hold him to her, rocking her hips to satiate the growing ache between her legs.

"Maggie," he rasped. "Maggie, my God." He had lifted her breasts from the low confines of her corset, and now sucked one nipple between his teeth. She quivered, and then almost arched off the bed as his fingers slid between her thighs to settle directly on a spot that was so exquisitely sensitive, it was almost painful.

"Shh," he murmured. "Trust me . . ." His palm flattened on her belly, and his thumb stroked softly, all over her sex. After the first shock, it was only pleasure she felt, rippling though her body and limbs until she was shaking. She barely felt him nudge against her, his body easing into hers as his hips rocked against hers. Every time she tried to focus on the sensation, he bit down on her nipple or stroked her a little harder, and by the time she forced her eyes open, his thighs were flush against hers, and she could feel him deep inside her.

That was when he paused, and inhaled a long, ragged breath. "I'm trying to be gentle, love, but—"

The ache had only grown more demanding. She moved restlessly beneath him. "Don't stop, then."

His eyes burned. "I wasn't considering stopping." He kissed her, then pushed himself up on one arm. "Unless you tell me to," he added, beginning a slow back and forth motion. His thumb resumed teasing her. "Tell me if I hurt you."

"No," she managed to gasp before being carried away again on a new tide of sensation and pleasure. Her muscles seemed to have slipped out of her control. Her legs shook and clenched tighter around his. Her belly was drawing up into a tight ball—her fingers grasped futilely at his shoulders, trying to anchor herself—

And then she splintered. With a deep, primal pulse the

tension broke, ebbing and rising like waves lapping at a shore. Rhys's thrusts abruptly grew hard and fast, almost in time with the beat of her heart. He bared his teeth in a savage grin, kissed her hard, and drove deep inside her one last time.

She couldn't say whether they lay there twined about each other for a minute or an hour. With his head on her shoulder, his chest rising and falling rapidly against hers, and the glorious contentment of lovemaking running through her, Margaret could have stayed there all night. Vaguely she knew she couldn't, but the reasons why seemed so trivial. And she was going to marry this wonderful man, with his wry humor and deep honesty. Her lover—and soon, her husband.

"Were you really intrigued when I told you to go raise goats?" she asked, sifting her fingers through his long, wavy hair.

He frowned without opening his eyes. "Hmm? Oh yes. I knew then I had to have you."

"You did not."

"I did, and you may ask Clyve. I told him so that very evening."

"No," she protested again, but secretly entranced by the thought. She'd been in a very ill temper that night. "You will tempt me to abuse you for the rest of our marriage."

He gave her a wicked look from under his eyelashes. "I shall retaliate, until you are speechless with pleasure."

Margaret smiled and stretched. "As I said: you will tempt me unbearably."

"It is my new purpose in life." He kissed her again, and rolled off the bed. "But first, a toast." He pulled on a banyan and lit a candle from the fire. "I'll fetch some wine."

By the time he returned with wine and a plate of ham, she had gotten her corset laced again and located her shoes. She didn't want to go back to Carlisle House yet, but to stay the night here would be unpardonable; even Clarissa would be appalled.

"I've sent Bunter to fetch a coach." Rhys handed her a glass of wine. "We have perhaps an hour." He crawled back onto the bed and pulled her into his lap. "To my bride," he whispered.

"To our future," she countered.

"May it last for decades."

"In health and prosperity," she added.

"Precisely. Although there would be some benefits to austerity." He leered at her legs, bared to the knee.

"Shame!" she cried, laughing. "I like a little prosperity. I could never afford such shoes as this before." She wiggled her feet, shod in black and pink silk shoes with diamond buckles.

"I have no objection to the shoes," he replied. "Only to the dress." She laughed again, and he kissed her again and again, until he blindly set aside the wineglasses.

A tremendous banging echoed through the house. Margaret gasped and nearly tumbled off his lap. Rhys caught her easily, and kissed her as he laid her back on the pillows. "Don't move," he murmured against her lips. "I expect it's Clyve, he has no sense of timing at all."

She laughed, her arms still tangled around his neck. "Send him away and come back to me."

Between light kisses over her cheek and jaw, he grinned. "On second thought, he'll go away if we ignore it long enough."

Her smile was coyly pleased. "A clever fellow, that Clyve."

"Indeed." He applied himself to kissing her in earnest, having no interest in what Clyve had to say. Dimly he realized the pounding on the door had stopped, and even though he knew he had to return Margaret to Carlisle House, she was making such enticing little moans as he kissed his way down her throat. God, what was another hour, when she had accepted his proposal?

"Dowling!"

Rhys raised his head. Margaret blinked up at him, her blue eyes bright with desire, her skin rosy. "What?" she whispered, trying to pull him back.

"Shh." He touched his fingertip to her lips as the shout echoed outside again.

"Damn you, Dowling! Open this bloody door!"

His gaze met Margaret's. The color bled from her cheeks, and her eyes fluttered shut in resignation. "Francis," she breathed. "Curse him."

"A bit worse than Clyve, then," said Rhys, trying not to grimace.

She bit her lip. "Much." She hesitated. "I—I must warn you, he was not pleased we walked out in Vauxhall the other night. I doubt he'll be pleased to find me here."

"Ah." He sat up and reached for his shirt. "Should I fetch my sword?"

"No," she said with a sigh. "It might be best if you stay here and let me speak to him alone."

Rhys regarded her steadily. "Are you reconsidering your answer to my proposal?"

"No, but—"

He got up and stepped back into his breeches. "Then we shall see him together. I refuse to cower and hide behind my bride."

"It wouldn't be hiding," she protested as he continued getting dressed. Rhys shook out her gown and held it up, helping her back into it with considerably less pleasure than when he helped her out of it. "It would be simple prudence . . ."

"It wasn't the most prudent thing to whisk you away from Carlisle House tonight." He cupped one hand around her cheek. Durham's shouts could be heard at intervals, growing angrier and louder with each moment. "I'm not afraid of your brother."

"I never said I was *afraid* of him."

"We are engaged to be married," he said. "Do you regret making love?"

She blushed. "Not at all, but—"

"Excellent." He grinned dangerously. "We're going to do it a lot, because I found it sublime. And I couldn't be made to regret it even if your brother resorted to medieval instruments of torture."

Her face bright red, she turned her back to him as she pulled up her petticoats to retie her garters. But in the looking glass Rhys caught the curve of a satisfied smile on her lips. He admired the slim line of her exposed leg for a moment, and considered ignoring Durham's rude interruption just as he would have ignored Clyve or Eccleston at a moment like this.

But the duke kept pounding on the door, which was growing tiresome. Reluctantly he put on his waistcoat and buttoned it up as he looked for his shoes. Margaret was also dressed by now. She put her hand in his extended one, and he pulled her close. "Are you truly content, love?"

She gazed up at him with sparkling blue eyes. "I am."

He smiled and kissed her lightly on the mouth. "Thank

God. For I am mightily contented." It could not be better, in Rhys's opinion. She was clever and sensible, spirited but kind, lovely and passionate in bed. And rich—bloody, bloody rich. As they walked through the forlorn rooms, her hand nestled snugly in his, Rhys unconsciously sketched the repaired ceilings and restored furnishings in his mind. It was a bit remote from town, but the house would be a marvel if it were restored. He could let it at a handsome rent, and turn his attention to the Welsh lands. That was his real heritage, the seat of the earldom and the proper way for a nobleman to support himself. Perhaps cattle would succeed where the sheep had failed; already herds were driven from Wales to the markets south of the Thames to meet the growing city's demands.

And he would have Margaret as well. Just the thought of keeping her with him was enough to make his blood run faster and hotter. If only Durham hadn't chased her down. He might have kept her another few hours, and made love to her slowly, lingering over every lovely inch of her skin.

He opened the door, reminding himself to be gracious and humble. Durham wasn't much of a gentleman, but other than fussing about the walk in Vauxhall, he'd been a decent chap as far as Rhys was concerned. He made a small, polite bow. "Sir."

Durham glared at him. They were of a height, but the duke was down a stair. "Margaret," he said in a frigid tone. "There you are."

"Yes. Were you looking for me?"

The duke's glare could have cut stone at that query. Rhys cleared his throat. "I must beg your pardon, sir, for bringing her away from Carlisle House. I told her of the cupids falling from my ceiling, and she expressed a wish to see them."

"Cupids," repeated Durham.

"The plasterwork is crumbling to pieces, Francis," Margaret said quickly. "It really is quite sad—and just as promised, an actual cupid fell to the dining room floor as we walked through."

The duke looked right at Rhys. It was a black, murderous look, and he felt a sudden need to cast his motives and intentions in a better light. "It was a sign from the gods," he said lightly. "I fell to one knee and begged Miss de Lacey for the honor of her hand in marriage." He covered her hand, still on his arm, with his own. "Most happily, she has agreed."

"I have," said Margaret, beginning to beam again. God, how he loved that smile, especially when it was directed at him.

"You have." Durham didn't appear surprised by this, but then he must have suspected.

Margaret nodded happily. Rhys decided a little contrition was in order. "I apologize for any impropriety in my actions of late, sir. My only defense is love, coupled with a solemn vow to be more circumspect in the future."

Durham looked between the two of them and said nothing. "Aren't you going to wish us happy, Francis?" asked Margaret, still smiling. "You told me I would find someone to have me, and now I must admit you were right; what a happy day this should be for you, as well as for me."

"You're in love," said the duke carefully. "A love match."

"Very much so," replied Rhys.

"I see." Durham roused himself as if from a stupor. "I've come to take you home, Margaret. Miss Cuthbert was very confused about where you'd gone."

"Poor Miss Cuthbert," she exclaimed. "We became separated in the crowd at the masquerade." She turned to Rhys. "Good night, my lord," she said politely, as if she hadn't been sprawled almost naked in his bed just half an hour before.

"Good night, my darling." He kissed her knuckles again, stroking his finger the length of her palm until she sucked in her breath and gave him a simmering glance. "May I call upon you this week, Your Grace?"

Durham had already started toward his coach. At Rhys's question he froze mid-step, then slowly turned back. "Yes, Lord Dowling," he said. "You should. Margaret?" Without waiting for her, he climbed into the coach.

Reluctantly Rhys released her. "Only a few weeks until you're mine forever," he breathed.

"Endless," she murmured back. "Call on me."

"Of course."

He stood on the steps watching until the coach drove off, and walked to the edge of the drive to watch until it disappeared, heading back to Mayfair.

Then he let out a shout of triumph, and swung his fist in the air.

Chapter Ten

Rhys arrived in Berkeley Square several days later, brimming with satisfaction. Today would be the beginning of a new period in his life; he would finally put an end to the excruciating decade of disaster. He had called on the Duke of Durham the day after his tryst with Margaret, and the duke was accommodating, if not gracious. He paid that no mind; Margaret had warned him her brother wasn't best pleased by her choice, but had promised he wouldn't interfere. Rhys did his best to be humble and keep in mind that the duke was being protective because he cared for his sister, but it was still a rather unpleasant negotiation. It was a relief to conclude matters, shake the duke's hand, and rush off to spend an hour with his betrothed.

He walked up the steps of the Duke of Durham's gleaming new mansion and rapped the knocker smartly. By God, what a fine day it was. He was the most fortunate fellow in London, it seemed. Within an hour or so, he would be bound to Margaret in man's legal eyes, if not yet in God's eyes. He remembered the feel of her skin beneath his palm, and an unconsciously fierce smile crossed his face. His—in a matter of weeks, or even days.

And the money. His solicitor had looked over the contract sent by Durham, and confirmed all was in order. Rhys was tired of being dunned for unpaid bills, but he truly couldn't wait to begin building his estate back into what it should be. He pictured Margaret at Dowling Park, her pale beauty vivid and fresh amid the wild Welsh marches, and said a brief prayer of thanks to Clyve's mother for putting a middle-class spinster on her list of brides.

The butler opened the door and ushered him inside, through the corridors to the duke's study. There was a lingering smell of freshly cut sawdust, and a whiff of new paint. Rhys surveyed the interior of the house with the eyes of a man who would soon be hiring his own builders and decorators, and liked what he saw. Margaret made many of the choices in the house's completion, he knew, and he was quite pleased to see her taste was elegant and clean, preferring brightness over dark. There wasn't a single cupid to be seen. Damn, he was a fortunate man.

Durham was waiting. He was civil enough but had a curious air about him, a sharp tension that plucked at Rhys's attention. He tried not to let it bother him—he and Durham didn't need to be friendly relations—but he couldn't ignore it, either.

"Shall we get on with it?" he asked. "I hope to see Margaret once everything is signed."

The duke gave an odd twisted smile. "Of course." He led the way to his desk, where the necessary papers were laid out. Rhys seated himself with barely restrained triumph. This was everything he'd wanted: a wife he could love and desire, and a fortune to restore Dowling for the sons she would give him. Durham pushed the papers his way, and Rhys barely stopped himself from scribbling his name all over them in a blind rush so he could hurry off to Margaret. She must know he was here; would she be waiting for him?

"I made a few minor changes," said the duke idly. "I trust that won't cause a problem."

He nearly grinned and said "of course not," because almost nothing could keep him from signing these papers and securing Margaret's hand in marriage, but at the last second he really noticed the duke's expression. Durham watched him with a heavy-lidded gaze, his eyes hard and cold. He leaned back in his chair as if he hadn't a care in the world, but the hand on his knee was curled into a fist. Something coiled up in alarm within Rhys's breast. Durham did not look like a man pleased to be marrying off his spinster sister. He had more the look of a cardsharp about to rook a mark of everything he had.

Rhys did not intend to be the gullible mark. "Ah. If you'll be so kind as to allow me a moment to review them?"

Durham inclined his head and waved one hand. "By all means."

He forced himself to read each word of the tedious contract's first page. This was supposed to have been done already, any differences negotiated between his solicitor and the duke's. It was ungentlemanly to confront each other this way. He reminded himself Durham hadn't been a gentleman at all until very recently, and then made himself read even more carefully. Everything appeared normal, just as he had expected, just as Simpkins, his attorney, had told him it would be . . . until he reached the terms of the settlements.

There he found Durham's minor change. Instead of forty thousand pounds in hard currency, Miss Margaret de Lacey was endowed with only that clothing and jewelry she owned at the date of her marriage, plus five hundred pounds inherited from her father. Nothing else.

His breath roared in his ears. Christ. He had signed contracts, wanting to make the house ready for his bride. Hired workmen. Placed orders. Made commissions. It had all made perfect sense when he was poised to marry the greatest heiress in London this year, but now . . . He was ruined more completely than ever.

"A minor change?" he asked, affecting as calm a tone as Durham used.

The duke's smile was chilling. "A last-minute reconsideration. Surely you understand."

Rhys met his gaze, keeping his temper with great effort. "May I inquire into the cause of this reconsideration?"

"A mistake on my part."

"What did you mistake, sir?"

Any trace of smile, however cold or mocking, was gone from Durham's face now. "My sister deserves a husband who wants more than her money. She's not a willful ambitious beauty capable of pursuing her own pleasure while he does the same; she's not made to live a parallel life with a man she can neither trust nor respect. And she certainly shouldn't be misled by a calculating seducer."

His hands shook with fury. "Some might call this breach of promise, Your Grace," he bit out.

"Ah, breach. You intend to file a suit?" The duke's face was fierce with victory. "I suppose we could reach an agreement, as gentlemen. No doubt five thousand should atone for any expenses you may have incurred on unrealized expectations."

Then Rhys saw. Durham didn't trust him, or didn't want Margaret to marry him, or simply wanted to exercise his whim. Durham wanted him gone. He expected Rhys to put down the contract and bow out, abandoning his pursuit because the real prize, her dowry, was no longer available. Three weeks ago he would have probably done just that, back when he wasn't so sure running off to the Continent would be so bad a choice.

But now . . . Now he couldn't think of it. Now he knew what she looked like when she threw back her head and laughed with sheer joy. Now he knew how capable and sensible and intelligent she was. Now he knew how her arms felt around his neck, what her mouth tasted of, and how intoxicating it was to make love to her.

This was his choice, then. Margaret and her love, or five thousand pounds. A vision of Dowling Park crumbling into the ocean crossed his mind, and the hollow hallways of the London house falling into ruin. He imagined sliding into true poverty, no longer with a mask of gentility, and his stomach knotted.

But then there was Margaret. What sort of man would he be if he bowed out now? If he didn't sign the papers, what would she think of him? He couldn't betray her like that, even if doing so wouldn't have ripped out his own heart and left it to die on the duke's polished mahogany desk.

"If I sign this contract, I get Margaret and nothing else," he said, to be very certain. "If I stand up and walk away, you'll pay me five thousand."

Durham nodded once.

Slowly, Rhys reached for the pen. He dipped it in the ink, carefully tapping the excess away, and signed the contract with deliberate care. "If you would be so good, Durham." He pushed the contract across the table and held out the pen.

Durham didn't move. "You're a damned fool."

"Indeed. Your signature, sir." He kept his eyes trained on the page. After a moment Durham sat forward and reached for the contract. He watched the duke's hand as he stabbed the pen into the inkpot and then scrawled his name. Sunlight flashed off his gold signet as he reached for the pounce pot and poured it over the wet ink. Only then did Rhys let out his breath in a silent sigh. It was done. "I would like to set a date at once."

The duke sat back in his chair and watched Rhys with a probing glare. "How are you going to provide for my sister?"

A damned impertinent question, given how he had just crippled the life they might have led. "I won't question your business acumen, Your Grace, and will thank you not to question mine," he said through thin lips.

"If she's ill-treated, I'll ruin you."

"I'm already ruined, as you well know," he retorted acidly, even as the seed of worry sprouted. Would he be able to provide for a wife? Certainly not as Margaret deserved. It was one thing for her to proclaim herself indifferent to his lack of fortune when they both believed she had a large one of her own, and quite another for her to embrace his reduced circumstances for herself. He pictured her admiring the black and pink silk shoes, the diamond buckles glittering in the candlelight, and the worry blossomed into a chilling anxiety. Good God, had he arrogantly thrown away her fortune so blindly? Without asking her? Perhaps she wouldn't wish to marry him any longer, without the money.

"If you will excuse me, sir, I should like to visit my bride now." He got to his feet and gave a curt bow. "Good day."

Durham just inclined his head, eyes still sharp with suspicion. Rhys forced himself to walk calmly until he reached the corridor and was out of sight. He let out a shaky breath. His shirt stuck to his back, damp with perspiration. His mind seemed in shock, jumping from one frantic question to the next without fixing on any answer. He would have to cancel the order for roofing slate—cancel the furniture ordered for Maggie's sitting room—tell the artist there would be no wedding portrait—tell Maggie—tell Maggie. . .

God help him. He had to tell her she would be marrying into penury. If she still agreed to marry him at all.

He asked the footman where Miss de Lacey was. In the garden, was the reply, and Rhys followed the man out of the house. A number of servants were busy outside, pulling weeds and clearing ground for the new plantings she envisioned. His chest hurt; he could never give her that sort of garden at his house, not now. Fear and dread tore at him. Perhaps she was better off here. Perhaps he ought not even put the choice to her, for she might choose him.

He walked through the garden, his steps falling faster and faster until he was almost running. Ahead, almost by the arbor, he caught a glimpse of her flat straw bonnet, tied on with a bright green ribbon.

She looked up at his approach, but her happy smile faded at his expression. "What's wrong?" she asked at once, without any form of greeting.

Rhys took her by the hand and pulled her behind him, away

from the prying ears of servants. She threw down her basket and clapped her free hand to her hat, hurrying along with him. When they were quite alone, he stopped.

"Rhys, what is it?" she asked again, fully alarmed now.

"Do you love me?" he asked, grasping her arms.

"Do I—? Of course, you know I do," she protested.

He shook his head. "No. Not that playful, flirting way. *Do you love me?*"

Margaret gaped at him. His fingers dug into the softness inside her elbows, but she barely noticed for the intense, almost agonized, expression on his face. "I do," she replied quietly but firmly. "More than anyone or anything. Come what may, my heart is yours forevermore."

His fierce look faded, replaced by relief and a dawning smile. "Thank God. The only way I could have misplayed this . . . mistaken this . . . was if you didn't love me."

Margaret didn't know what to make of that. "Misplayed?" she repeated. "Is there some—some game I do not understand here?"

A vaguely bitter smile crossed his face. "A game. Yes, I do believe it has been a contest."

She frowned. "What are you talking about?" A terrible thought struck her. "Does this involve my brother?"

"Yes."

Her heart fell a thousand feet. Francis had refused. After all she had said and sworn to him, her brother hadn't given his consent. "I will tear his bloody head off," she said venomously. "I will make him rue the day he ever considered contravening my wishes—"

"We signed the marriage contract," he told her. "Just now. I hope you can assemble your trousseau quickly, for I have no patience for a long betrothal."

For the second time in minutes, Margaret stared at him, speechless. "What?" she cried. "He—You—he consented? We are truly to be married?"

"Of course." He grinned at her. "Did you think I would be denied?" And he kissed her. Margaret felt the ground shift beneath her feet, as it always did when his lips touched her. For a while all thought of Francis faded away; who cared for brothers . . . or really anything but Rhys . . . at a moment like this?

"But then why did you look so grim?" she asked several minutes later, when her head had cleared. "Are—are you suffering doubts?"

"Doubts," he repeated, holding her close. One hand moved soothingly over her back, but then he released her and turned away. "Perhaps. Not for myself, but . . . We did play a little game, your brother and I."

"A game?" She hovered anxiously beside him. "What sort of game?"

He sighed. "A game where we . . . tested each other."

"Test? What sort of test?" She was instantly suspicious again. "What did he do?"

He traced one fingertip down the lines between her brows until they smoothed away. "You have no dowry, Maggie," he whispered.

"What?" That made no sense. Everyone knew Francis had promised her forty thousand pounds. But Rhys kept stroking her face, and it was hard to keep up any outrage while he was touching her. "That's ridiculous," she murmured.

"The contract I signed specified that you had no dowry," he said. "Nothing but the clothes and jewels you already own."

"But—but you'd be ruined," she said. "Your plans—your hopes— How can you call that a test?"

"He didn't think I loved you," he said simply. "He thought I was an opportunist, a scoundrel who wanted you only for the money. So he prepared a contract that made it very clear I could have you, and only you. The only money I would have from him would be five thousand pounds, if I agreed to walk away without you."

"That is not a game!" she cried, his meaning finally sinking in.

"No, I rather think it was." He gathered her close again. "And I won," came his whisper in her ear. "He shall keep his money, but I shall have you. And that, my darling, makes me far richer."

"Then—why did you speak of doubts? Did you doubt I would still marry you?" She pushed against his chest until she could look into his face.

She had never seen him look so grave. "I wouldn't blame you if you jilted me," he said. "I can never offer you this." He waved one hand to indicate the grounds and house behind them. "I have an empty town house and a crumbling Welsh manor. I can't offer you a fashionable life in London. You would be a fool to marry me now."

"And if I didn't," she said faintly. "Would you marry one of those other ladies on Clyve's list?"

"No." The color seemed to have leached from his face. "Alpine goats have more appeal than they do."

She sniffed, then gasped, then choked on a horrified laugh. "You can't mean it."

He didn't laugh or even smile. "You could marry someone Durham approves of. You could keep your place in life."

Margaret thought of the polished floors and soaring ceilings of Durham House, the rooms decorated to her own taste, and imagined having such a house of her own to set up and manage. Of the balls she could continue to attend, the fashionable clothing she could continue ordering, the society she could keep. And she thought of Rhys returning alone to his bare house, his steps echoing in the empty rooms, with more cupids falling from the ceiling. Of the witless idiots who would mock him and sneer at him for failing to marry an heiress. Of the fact that he had signed a marriage contract that condemned him to even deeper ruin, since now he would have a wife to support—because he loved her.

"I think I would rather herd goats with you than marry another man," she said. He stared at her a moment, then his shoulders eased as if a cord had been cut. "I have been poor for most of my life," she went on. "These few months as sister of a duke have been like a dream, but not always a happy one. Every moment with you, though . . . those have been happy. Somehow we will find a way. I would rather be poor with you than wealthy with another man."

His eyes closed. "Maggie," he whispered. "Darling, I'm sorry—"

"Shh." She rose up on her toes to touch her lips to his.

"Don't be." It was Francis's fault, not Rhys's, but she wasn't interested in that right now. "If you love me, kiss me again."

His smile was slow but real. "How many times, Miss de Lacey?"

"As many as you can manage."

"And for how long, Miss de Lacey?" he murmured, his lips brushing hers.

She put her arms around his neck. "For the rest of my life."

CHAPTER ELEVEN

Margaret knocked at her brother's study door. As she waited, she adjusted the cuffs on her traveling dress. The footmen were bringing down her trunks and taking them out to the wagon waiting in the street. She just had one last thing to do before she left forever. When the servant opened the door, she went inside.

"I've come to say good-bye, Francis," she said calmly to her brother.

He scowled back. Since the day Rhys signed the contract, Francis had been surly and curt to everyone. He looked as if he hadn't slept in days, and a glass of sack was never far from his hand. Today the whole decanter of wine sat at his elbow. "You're leaving?"

"I am. Before I go, I wish to say a few words to you."

He hesitated, then jerked his head in a single nod. Margaret waved the servant away, waiting until the fellow closed the door behind him. She turned back to her brother. "You, sir, are a snake."

His eyebrows drew together sullenly, but he didn't reply.

"Perhaps you think you did the right thing." She shrugged. "You never bothered to tell me one word about what you planned to do, or why, so I don't know what justification you made to yourself. Instead you took back all your money, which was your right—I told you to keep it from the start. I do not hold it against you, nor do I want it back. But instead of being a gentleman and a man of your word, you lied to Rhys, and for that I will never forgive you."

"I thought he only wanted the money," her brother muttered. He took a gulp of his wine. "He's a damned fortune hunter, Meg."

"He's the man I love," she flung back at him. "An earl, a respected and responsible man—and no different in fortune from every other man who courted me. What did you expect, when you told the world I would have forty thousand pounds for a dowry?"

A muscle in his jaw flexed. He stared into his glass. "I didn't think you would be swayed by a tawdry seduction. You fell for him too quickly, Meg. Wait a year and I'll restore the funds, if he's still the one you want."

"Wait a year?" She laughed in scorn. "What is another year to Margaret, who's already waited three decades to find a man who could find her beautiful? Interesting? Desirable? I'd rather have Rhys and take in washing than wait a year merely to appease some suspicious whim of yours."

"Will he still find you beautiful when his credit dries up and he can't rebuild his estate?" Francis growled. "Will you still love him when your fine clothes have worn to rags?"

She raised her chin. "I will," she said quietly. "I have been poor and plainly dressed before; I shall survive it again. Rhys has lived in his estate as it is, and is content to continue doing so." She paused. "I'm sorry you can't see that we truly care for each other, but I'm happy with my decision."

Her brother swilled back the considerable wine in his glass. "I don't want you to make a mistake, Meg," he said thickly, looking almost gaunt with despair. "He's seduced you—you must wait until the allure wears off. It will, I promise you. Better to suffer a bit of heartbreak now than years of regret, knowing you threw away your chance to be happy . . ."

When he said no more, she bit her lip in sudden understanding. "Someone broke your heart," she guessed. He closed his eyes. "I never knew," she said softly. "Oh, Francis—"

"Leave it," he snapped. "It was a youthful mistake, and not one I'll make again."

"Yes, like the way you gave up all spirits after your first blue-deviled morning."

"Marriage is far more important than that!" he roared, erupting out of his chair with such fury, she took a step backwards in alarm. "And more lasting. If you regret it and wish to come home in six months, there is nothing I can do! You will never be free of him."

There was an element of torment in his voice she'd never heard before and didn't quite understand. "I don't want to be free of Rhys," she said slowly. "Francis, I love him. He loves me. No matter what lies ahead for us, I trust him to be honorable, just as I vow to be with him. I'm not a schoolgirl any longer, with vague dreams of marriage that can't possibly bear up in life. In truth, perhaps it's better I'm a more mature woman. I suspect many bad marriages are born out of youth's naivety and idealism."

His mouth quirked in a bitter smile. "Too right you are, Meg. Too right." He sighed. "Perhaps you're right. You're not a silly girl. I still think of you as a child, but of course you are not. And I daresay you've always been more level-headed than I in any event."

Margaret hesitated. He looked older, beaten down, and tired. For the first time she realized he had lost weight since becoming the duke. His clothing, fine and elegant though it was, hung a bit on his tall frame. It occurred to her that he would be alone in this enormous mansion after she left, weighed down by duties and responsibilities without a single friend or trusted relative to lean on and confide in. It wasn't like Francis to lean on anyone, but she felt a burst of compassion for him anyway. "I hope you won't allow one mistake to keep you from ever risking love again. You would make a splendid husband."

He stared out the window for a moment. "I highly doubt it."

"Because you were wrong once? Or because you cannot trust the motives of anyone who would want to marry a duke?"

He shot her a sour look, then sighed, his gaze sweeping the room. "I suppose I have to consider it, for the sake of all this."

"For your own sake, consider it," she said firmly. "And for mine. I look forward to spoiling your children."

A bit of real humor softened his expression. "They had better be sons. A daughter would destroy me. You've come damned close, and you're only a sister."

Margaret laughed. "Yes, sons! I wish you several sons, so you might reap the full measure of your sex's pig-headedness."

Francis smiled faintly. "Of course you would." He turned back to the window. The grounds behind Durham House had been sadly neglected, and were still a mess of dug up landscape. "This isn't mine, not really. It's only mine to administer until the next generation comes along." He paused, then said quietly, almost to himself, "Until my son inherits it."

"First you need the wife." She came up and straightened his lace jabot, flicking her hands over his velvet-clad shoulders. "A good, sensible lady who won't dissolve in tears when you roar at her. Someone who can bring warmth and laughter to the house even when you're in one of your grim moods. Someone who will make a good mother."

He grunted. "How will I find such a creature, if you leave?"

"Miss Cuthbert is still available to assist you in finding a match," she offered, but he only looked at her grimly. She rolled her eyes. "Think of it as a lucrative investment. You never have any trouble finding those. And this time you shall have additional pleasures not found on the 'Change."

He started to smile, then frowned. "Did Dowling—?"

"Did I what?" Rhys spoke from the doorway. Neither of them had heard it open, although a flustered servant hovered just behind him. His dark gaze rested on Margaret, steady and warm, before shifting to the duke. "Your Grace." He bowed. "Miss de Lacey."

She couldn't help it; a wide smile spread across her face, and she managed to walk sedately to his side even though she wanted to run and throw her arms around him. "Lord Dowling is late for his bride," she said lightly.

"Lord Dowling is ever so grateful she waited for him," he replied, catching up her hand to kiss her knuckles. "I had a small errand to do."

"Where are you going?" growled Francis.

"To the church," Rhys said. "It's our wedding day."

Her brother seemed startled. She saw the dismay in his face before he masked it behind a scowl and grumbled something under his breath. "Won't you come with us?" she asked on impulse. "Will you come to my wedding, Francis?"

"I don't approve of this," he muttered.

"That has been made abundantly clear," said Rhys, squeezing Margaret's hand. "But we would still be honored to have you stand up with us."

The duke regarded them for a moment, then jerked his head. "Very well then."

Durham was silent and glowered at him the entire way to the church, but Rhys barely felt it. He knew it made Margaret happy to have her brother there, even if he had treated them so abominably. He didn't quite have it in him to forgive the duke so readily, but for Margaret's sake, he could hold his tongue today.

The wedding was brief and small. Clarissa Stacpoole and Freddie Eccleston came, and Clyve was there. Aside from a loud, indrawn breath when Margaret repeated her vows, Durham said nothing during the ceremony. Margaret's eyes grew wide when Rhys slid the ring on her finger, a wide gold band with a clear blue aquamarine set on it. He grinned at her in reply, and her answering smile was brilliant with happiness.

When the ceremony was over, Clarissa provided enough chatter for them all, although Clyve and Eccleston did contribute hearty congratulations. Margaret murmured an excuse to her friend and walked to where her brother stood apart from the rest.

"Can you be happy for me, Francis?" she asked softly. "For I am very happy."

He kept his eyes fixed away from her. "I shall try. I suppose it will be easier if Dowling treats you properly."

"I have no doubts. I believe—" Through the open church door, Margaret caught sight of a familiar and expected figure. "Pardon," she said to her brother, and hurried forward to meet Miss Cuthbert.

"Am I late?" cried her companion. Her cheeks were flushed, and her hair was escaping its cap. "Oh dear, I've missed the wedding!"

"But not the congratulations." Margaret pressed her hand. "We missed you."

A fierce smile broke out on the older woman's face. "I had a good reason, Miss de Lacey—or no, you are my Lady Dowling now! But here it is. I did my best." She handed over a heavy purse.

Rhys had come up beside her. "What's this?"

"My wedding gift to you." Margaret gave it to him with a smile. "Since I could not provide Alpine goats."

He looked inside, then sharply back at her. "'Tis money."

"Nearly a thousand pounds," whispered Miss Cuthbert. "All that lovely silk brought a pretty penny!"

"My gowns," Margaret explained to her astonished husband. "I won't need them in Wales anyway."

"You sold your gowns?" Francis sounded outraged. "What were you thinking?"

"That there are more important things than clothes," she told him.

"If ever I doubted my infinite riches in wedding you, this would remove them forever," Rhys said. "I do so love a sensible woman."

"And beautiful," piped up Clarissa.

"Beyond compare," agreed Rhys, eyes twinkling at his new wife.

"You are released from your employment, Miss Cuthbert," said Francis. "You were shamefully neglectful of your duties." The lady's chin trembled, but she merely curtseyed.

"I shall provide the highest possible character reference," Margaret told her.

"As will I." Clarissa gave Francis a withering look. "And my mother, who is, as you know, the most well-known gossip in all London. You shall be turning offers away for years, Miss Cuthbert."

"Thank you, my dear." And Miss Cuthbert actually smiled.

"I'm surrounded by traitors," said Francis heavily.

"All idiots are," Margaret replied. "Accept it and be gracious. Will you send me off with a kiss?"

"You're leaving now?"

"Yes." Rhys laced his fingers through Margaret's. "I've closed up my house in town, and we depart this very day. It's a long journey to Wales."

Clarissa began to sob. "Oh—oh, Margaret—I'm going to miss you so!"

The travel coach was waiting outside. Margaret bade everyone goodbye before turning to her brother. She put her hands on his shoulders and kissed his cheek. "Be happy," she whispered. "I wish you as much love as I found."

He never replied. As she and Rhys settled into the seats, and waved out the windows until Clarissa's sobs couldn't be heard and Miss Cuthbert's fluttering handkerchief was lost in the sea of passersby, Margaret waited for some sign from her brother. But he never flinched, and just as the church vanished from sight, he turned and walked away.

"Are you very sorry?" Rhys finally asked when she sat back.

She sighed. "A little. But not sorry enough to give him his way."

"Are you happy, then?"

"Blissfully." She touched the ring. "Where did you get this? I didn't expect one."

"A happy oversight. When I sold everything, this was judged not worth selling, so it was left in the bank." A note of apology entered his voice. "'Tis only an aquamarine, not a sapphire."

"It's perfect. I could not ask for a better wedding gift."

At the mention of gift, her husband weighed the purse in one hand. "A good number of goats could be purchased with this."

"Or cattle." She grinned. "Or cupids. You know, I think you should consider parceling off the London property; there aren't enough decent houses as it is, and now everyone wants to move west. And take a tenant for the house. Look how Mrs. Cornelys improved Carlisle House."

"You've got it all worked out, haven't you," he said in amusement.

"Not at all! But since you liked my idea about tending goats so much—"

He hauled her across the seat to kiss her soundly. "Enough about the goats. Let's think of some happier ideas for enduring this journey across England."

She smiled up at him. "I'm sure we'll do very well, between the two of us."

Epilogue

Four months later

The thick letter didn't look extraordinary. It was posted from Holborn, with no indication of its import.

"What can this be?" Rhys held it up questioningly. "An acquaintance of yours?"

Margaret read the name. "No. I've no idea."

He broke the seal and began to read as Margaret slipped a bite of bacon under the table to the stray dog she'd adopted. The poor thing had been living in the stables, but seemed to recognize Margaret as his saving angel. He was never far from her feet.

They had settled into life in Wales rather easily. The house had been spared the infestation of cupids, and, aside from the crumbling east wing, was habitable once the roof was patched and the burned timbers cleared from the front façade. Rhys plunged back into managing his lands, and now flocks of sheep covered the hills—not his own sheep, but tenants'. In the spring he would be paid a harvest of lambs, to begin anew, and this time, he vowed to Margaret, they wouldn't be grazed in any low-lying areas.

It felt almost right to sink back into the economy she had practiced before the Durham inheritance upended her life. Margaret paid her own accounts again, did her own mending, and tended her own kitchen garden. She supposed it would horrify the people who had invited her to their balls and masquerades in London, but she rather liked the days, with her duties beyond what dress to wear, and even more so the nights, when Rhys returned home to make love to her with very unfashionable passion. He laughed that they would have been thrown out of society sooner or later anyway, for he couldn't keep his hands off her, which was simply not done by earls.

Even with that economy upon them, though, there was always a little bacon to spare for the dog. She would have to think of a name for him, since he didn't appear to be running off any time soon. Not that any dog she'd ever met would run away from bacon. She was feeding him another tiny tidbit when Rhys said her name.

"Maggie," he said blankly. "*Maggie.*"

"What is it?" She got up and rushed around the table to read over his shoulder, only to gasp aloud.

Francis was paying her dowry, in full. Even more, he had provided a separate dower for her, including a choice property in Cavendish Square in London. The letter was from the attorney laying out the terms, and included documents for Rhys to sign in acceptance.

"He relented," she said softly.

"He did indeed," Rhys muttered, scanning through the

documents. "To a generous degree." He turned over the last page, and a folded separate letter fluttered out. "This is for you," he said, handing it to her.

Margaret unfolded the paper. *I was wrong*, it read simply, in Francis's sharp, bold writing. *I wish you every happiness.* Her throat felt tight, and she gave a little gasp as her eyes filled with tears. That meant more to her than the money. Every month she'd written to him about her new life, but he never responded, until now. She'd missed her brother.

"I see I shall have to add Durham to my prayers after all," said Rhys gently, watching her. "If he's made you smile, I cannot hate him."

"No, don't hate him," she said, dabbing at her eyes. She was glad to have her brother's blessing at last, but his funds were very welcome as well. "Bless him with every breath, for now we shall have a new roof."

Her husband stared at her for a moment, then threw back his head and laughed. "And a goat! We can name him Francis." He pulled her into his lap. "How does it feel to be a wealthy woman?"

She smiled up at him. His skin was even darker now that he spent his days outside again, but his eyes still twinkled as wickedly as ever at her. "Lovely. Although not half as wonderful as it feels to be loved by you."

The Duke of Durham has a scandalous secret, long-buried but not completely forgotten. And after a lifetime of waiting, it's about to emerge to haunt his three sons, who each have to risk everything to discover The Truth About The Duke.

Neither wealth nor beauty will help Lady Francesca Gordon rescue her underage niece Georgiana from a cruel and selfish stepmother. Only London's best solicitor can win her custody of the girl. But when Edward de Lacey, son of the powerful Duke of Durham, hires away the one man who can do the job, Francesca decides that Edward himself must champion her case . . . if only she can win over the dashing lord's stony-walled heart.

But Edward has reason to be guarded: London's tabloids have just exposed his father's secret first marriage, throwing both his inheritance and his engagement into jeopardy. Yet when Francesca offers a one-of-a-kind chance to undo the newspapers' damage, Edward is forced to agree to a partnership . . . and now, each moment together feeds the flames of his scandalous longing for the passionate, sensitive widow. But when Georgiana disappears, fate hands them the ultimate test—leaving their fragile love hanging in the balance.

Read on for a sneak peek at *One Night in London* by Caroline Linden, coming in September 2011 from Avon

The Duke of Durham was dying.

It wasn't spoken of openly, but everyone knew. With quiet steps and whispered instructions the servants were already preparing for the mourning. The solicitor had been sent for. Letters had been urgently dispatched to the duke's other sons, one in the army and one in London, summoning them home. Durham himself knew his death was nigh, and until a sudden attack of heart pains the previous evening, he had been approving the funeral arrangements personally.

Edward de Lacey watched his father doze, the gaunt, stooped figure propped up on pillows in the bed as he struggled to breathe. The doctor had assured him there was no hope, and that the end was swiftly approaching. Edward would be very sorry to lose his father, but there was no question that the duke's time on earth was spent.

Durham stirred. "Charles?" he said faintly. "Is that you?"

Edward moved forward. "No, sir," he said quietly. "Not yet."

"I must . . . speak . . . to Charles," his father gasped. "Need . . . to—" He raised one hand and clutched weakly at Edward's sleeve. "Get Charles . . . you must."

"He's on his way," promised Edward, although he wasn't sure of any such thing. He'd filled the letter to his brother with the direst language possible, but that could only have any effect after the letter found its way into Charlie's hands, and even then Charlie might be too drunk to understand that he must come home immediately, let alone actually make the journey. Edward clasped his father's hand between his own and expressed his hope, rather than his expectation. "He will surely be here at any moment."

"I have to tell him . . ." Durham mumbled fretfully. "All of you . . ."

Edward waited, but his father just closed his eyes, looking anguished. Unwillingly Edward felt a flicker of petty annoyance; always Charlie, the firstborn, even though Edward was the son who was always there when the duke wanted him. He shoved it aside. It was unworthy to think such a thought as his father sank closer and closer to mortality. "Tell me, sir," he whispered. "I will tell Charlie in the event . . ." *In the event he doesn't arrive in time.* "I will make sure he knows as soon as he arrives, if you should be asleep then."

"Yes . . ." came the duke's soft, slurred voice. "Sleep. Soon. But not . . . without . . . telling Charles . . ." He sighed, and went so still Edward feared the worst for a moment, until the faint rise of his father's chest proved him still alive.

In the utter quiet of the room, a distant drumming sounded. Hooves pounding hard up the gravel drive, Edward realized, at the same moment his father bolted upright in bed. "Charles," croaked the duke, his face ashen. "Charles—is it he, Edward?"

Edward rushed to the window in time to see the rider's

scarlet coat before he flashed out of sight beneath the portico in front of the house. "It's Gerard, Father."

"Ah," said Durham, slumping once more into his pillows. "A good boy, Gerard."

Edward smiled wryly at his father's masked disappointment. He was glad his younger brother, at least, was home. "I'll go fetch him right up."

"Do that," murmured Durham. "I will be glad to see him. And Charles . . . Charles will be here soon?"

"At any moment," Edward said again as he slipped through the door and held it for the doctor to take his place in the room. He reached the top of the stairs just as his brother came running up.

"Am I too late?" demanded Gerard.

Edward shook his head.

Gerard exhaled and ran one hand over his head. His dark hair was damp with sweat, and dust covered him from head to toe. "Thank God. I've been riding all day; probably damn near killed the poor horse." He glanced at Edward. "Charlie?"

"No sign of him, as usual," muttered Edward as they walked down the hall. "Father's been calling for him for two days now."

"Well, some things never change." Gerard sighed and pulled loose a few buttons of his coat. "I should wash."

Edward nodded. "I had all the rooms prepared. But Gerard—hurry."

His brother paused on the threshold of his bedchamber. "He's really dying, then?"

It did seem incredible, even to Edward. Durham had been a vital person, every bit as robust and daring as his sons. Since the death of the duchess over twenty years ago, the household had been a preserve of male pursuits, and no one pursued them harder than Durham himself. Edward was almost eighteen before any of the brothers could outshoot their father, and they outrode him only when the doctor flatly ordered His Grace out of the saddle at the age of seventy after a bad fall injured his back.

But now Durham was over eighty. He was an old man, and had been dying for the better part of a year. Gerard just hadn't seen the decline. "Yes, he's really dying," Edward said in answer to his brother's question. "I would be surprised if he lasts the night."

When his younger brother slipped into the sickroom a few minutes later, Edward had already returned to his post by the window. Durham had told him to wait there, to announce the moment Charlie arrived. He wondered what his father wanted so desperately to tell Charlie; God knew Charlie hadn't cared much for anything the duke had had to say for the last ten years or so, and apparently still didn't. But whatever final words Durham had for his heir, they were obviously of tremendous importance. When he heard the creak of the door at Gerard's entrance, Durham lurched up again and cried out, "Charles?"

"No, Father, 'tis Gerard." Not a trace of offense or upset marred Gerard's soft tone. He crossed to the bed and took his father's hand. "Edward wrote me some nonsense that you were ill," he said. "I came to thrash some sense into him."

"But why did you not bring *Charles?*" whispered the duke in anguish. "Ah, lads. I have to tell Charles . . . ask his forgiveness . . ."

That was new. Edward abandoned his window post as Gerard shot him a curious look. "Forgiveness, Father?"

A tear leaked from the duke's eye, tracing a glistening path down his sunken cheek. "I must beg pardon of you all. I didn't know . . . If only I had known, in time . . . You, Gerard, will come out well enough—you always do—and Edward will have Lady Louisa . . . But Charles—Charles will not know what to do . . ."

"What do you mean?" Edward had to admire his brother's calm, even tone. The duke's demeanor was raising the hair on the back of his neck.

"Edward . . ." Durham reached feebly for him, and Edward stepped forward. He knelt beside the bed, leaning closer to hear the duke's quavering voice. "I know you would forgive me, and even know what to do . . . Forgive me, I should have told you earlier . . . before it was too late . . ."

"Told me what, Father? What is too late?" Edward fought down a surge of apprehension. Behind his back, Gerard hissed quietly at the doctor to leave.

"Tell Charles . . ." rasped the duke. An ominous rattle echoed in his breath. "Tell Charles . . . I am sorry."

"You will tell him yourself when he arrives," Edward said. Gerard crossed the room in two strides, but shook his head as he gazed out the window facing the road from London. Edward turned back to his father. "Rest yourself, sir."

"Rest!" Durham coughed, his entire body convulsing. "Not until you grant me forgiveness . . ." His blue eyes were almost wild as he stared at Edward.

"I—" Edward stared. "Yes. Whatever it is, Father, I forgive you."

"Gerard," cried the duke.

"You know I will forgive you, sir." Gerard had come back to the bed. "But for what sin?" Even he couldn't joke now.

"I tried . . ." The duke's voice faded. "The solicitor . . . will tell . . . Sorry . . ."

Durham never spoke with any clarity again. He slipped in and out of consciousness the rest of the day and night, and finally breathed his last in the darkest hour of the night. Edward slumped in the chair next to the bed and listened to the silence when the tortured breathing finally stopped. Gerard had been sitting with him until a few hours ago, when he finally went to bed, exhausted from his hard ride. The doctor had long since dozed off, and Edward saw no reason to wake him, either. Durham had lived a long and full life, and suffered the last several months of it in pain. It was a kindness that he was at peace now.

Slowly he levered himself upright in the chair and leaned forward to take his father's hand. It was still warm; it felt just as it had for the last year or so, when the wasting illness had taken hold of the duke and shriveled his flesh. But there was no strength in it, and never would be again. "Fare thee well, Father," he said quietly, and laid the limp hand back on his father's chest.

The duke's solicitor, Mr. Pierce, arrived the following day. He had handled the Durham affairs for twenty years, as his father and grandfather had done before him. Edward was waiting in the front hall when his carriage pulled up to the steps.

"I see I should begin with condolences," Pierce said, glancing at the black crepe already on the door. "I am very sorry for your loss, my lord."

"Thank you." Edward bowed his head.

"His Grace sent full instructions, as always. I was delayed a day, gathering everything he wished me to provide you." Pierce paused. "I will be available as soon as you wish, of course."

"My brother, Lord Gresham, is not yet here. Captain de Lacey and I are in no hurry to proceed without him."

Pierce nodded. "As you wish, sir."

"There is just one thing." Edward raised one hand. "My father was quite agitated near the end, begging us to forgive him, but he wouldn't say for what sin. He said you would explain."

Pierce looked startled. "He didn't—he didn't tell you?"

"Tell us what?" Gerard was coming down the stairs, buttoning his scarlet jacket.

"Welcome home, Captain. My deepest sympathies," said the solicitor with a quick bow.

"Thank you, Mr. Pierce." Gerard turned to Edward. "The mysterious sin?" Edward nodded once, and Gerard fixed his penetrating gaze on Mr. Pierce again. "Do you know what Durham meant by that?" he asked in his usual direct way.

Mr. Pierce's eyes darted between the two of them. "Yes," he said. "I believe I do. I have a letter, as well as many other documents from His Grace, which will explain everything—as much as can be explained. But I think we should await Lord Gresham so that you might hear it, and the contents of His Grace's will, together."

"God only knows when Gresham will find his way out to Sussex," said Gerard. "My brother and I would like to know now."

"Yes," Edward said when the solicitor shot a questioning look at him. He and Gerard had been unable to guess what Durham meant, and it was bothering Gerard as much as it was him. Over breakfast they agreed that since Durham had pushed the task onto the solicitor, it was undoubtedly some matter of inheritance. Perhaps their father had imposed some onerous conditions in his will or made some unexpected bequests—but that, of all things, was something completely in Durham's power to change, and have no need of forgiveness. They were both at a complete loss, and very impatient to know the answer.

Mr. Pierce drew in a deep breath. "His Grace wished you to hear it at once—all three of you, since it affects you all."

"Now, Mr. Pierce," snapped Gerard.

"If you please," Edward added more politely. "On this we do not wish to wait."

"Your father—"

"Is dead," said Edward. "I believe you are in my brother's employ now—at the moment."

Everyone knew Edward ran Durham, right down to which flowers were planted in the gardens. Everyone knew Charles, the new duke, wouldn't give a damn which solicitor handled his affairs. If Edward wanted to sack Pierce, Charles wouldn't lift a finger in protest. And Mr. Pierce knew just how profitable it was to handle Durham's legal affairs. He hesitated only a moment, glancing from Edward to Gerard and back.

"The trouble is," the solicitor began in a lowered voice, "it is not a well-defined problem; it stems from events many, many years ago, and unwinding the knot after so long has proven very difficult."

"What knot?" growled Gerard.

"There is a chance," said Mr. Pierce, as though choosing each word with care, "a very small, *remote* possibility, although it is impossible to ignore, that . . ."

"What?" prompted Edward sharply when the man hesitated again. This was doing nothing to ease his bad feeling about anything.

"That you—all of you, I mean—may . . . not be . . . able to receive your . . . full inheritances."

"What?"

"Explain." Edward held up one hand to quell Gerard's outburst. "Why not?"

Mr. Pierce winced at his cold tone. "His Grace was married before he wed your late mother, the duchess," he said, almost whispering. "Long ago." He paused. "He and the young lady both decided the marriage had been a rash, youthful mistake and they parted ways." Another pause. "But . . . there was no divorce."

He didn't need to say more. The implications came at Edward in a blinding rush. He looked at his brother, whose expression reflected his own dawning horror. Holy God. If Durham had been married . . . If his first wife had still survived when he married again . . . when he married *their mother*. . .

The solicitor was still speaking. "Unfortunately, recent letters received by the duke made clear this marriage was not as forgotten as His Grace had believed, and implied the woman might still be alive. His Grace expended a great deal of effort and expense trying to locate her—".

"Are you saying," said Gerard in an ominous voice, "our father was a *bigamist?*"

A fine flush of perspiration broke out on Mr. Pierce's forehead. "That has not been proved."

"But it is a distinct possibility." Gerard stabbed one finger at the man. "And you didn't tell us!"

"I was expressly ordered not to, sir!"

"What do the letters say?" demanded Edward. He felt struck numb. It was one thing for Gerard not to have known; Gerard had been on the Iberian Peninsula until two months ago, and then with his regiment at Dover. It was even understandable that Durham would have kept it from Charlie, even though he was the heir apparent. Charlie wouldn't have taken it well, or been much help in getting to the root of the problem. But his father had kept this dreadful secret from *him*, from the son who had stayed at his side and managed his estates and dined with him every evening and cared for him in his final illness. Of all the people Durham might have trusted enough to confide in, Edward thought he would have been the one.

Apparently, he was wrong.

"I have brought them, as His Grace instructed." Mr. Pierce indicated his bulging satchel apologetically. "I believe he wished to take care of the problem himself and spare all three of you any uneasiness, my lord."

Great lot of good that did, thought Edward bitterly. "We'll look at them later," he said, masking his emotions with effort. The butler stepped forward at his wave.

"Thank you, my lord," said Pierce with a bow. He followed the butler up the stairs, his relief evident in his quick step. Edward strode after his brother, who had turned and left the hall. Gerard was already pouring a drink when Edward stepped into the drawing room.

"The bloody scoundrel," muttered Gerard.

"Father, or the solicitor?" He closed the doors behind him. No need to titillate the servants further.

"Both." Gerard swallowed his brandy in one gulp and poured another. He raised one eyebrow at Edward, who shook his head. "But mostly Father, I suppose. What the bloody hell was he thinking?"

"I have no idea, and I was right here all the time."

His brother glanced at him, apology flickering in his eyes. "I didn't mean that. Just . . . What kind of fool keeps that secret?"

"A fool who doesn't want to look like one," said Edward. "Or an old fool who still thinks he can control everything."

"Bastards," Gerard said, and Edward flinched at the word spoken aloud. "We'll be bastards if this woman turns up alive. All this" —he swept one hand around to indicate the room, the house, the estate— "will go to someone else." He paused. "To whom would it go? I can't even recall."

Edward sighed, not wanting to think about that. Durham was supposed to go to Charlie. "Some distant cousin. Augustus, I suppose."

"Perhaps he's the one who sent those letters," said Gerard.

"Perhaps. Perhaps it's the woman herself. Perhaps her children. Good God," he said as the thought struck him. "You don't suppose Father had other children?"

"Wouldn't that cause a stir?" His brother gave a harsh crack of laughter. "Rather odd they haven't come forward in all this time."

"Rather odd our own father never mentioned the possibility of their existence." Edward walked to the tall windows that overlooked the lush gardens his mother had designed and planted, and he himself had maintained. He felt at home in those gardens, at peace—usually. A hot fury burned in his chest that all this might be yanked out from beneath him and given to another. He had spent his life here, doing everything that was needed. He was needed here. Without Durham, what would he be, where would he go? How could he face his fiancée, Lady Louisa Halston, and tell her he was no longer Lord Edward de Lacey, brother of the Duke of Durham, but just some bastard son with no property? The scandal over his father's bigamy would be enormous. How could he ask Louisa to endure that gossip? It simply staggered the mind, that Durham had kept a prior marriage secret, knowing it could have come to light at any time and upended everything in their lives. In that moment, Edward was almost glad the duke was dead, because he would have surely doomed himself to hell for what he would say to his father now.

Gerard had come up beside him. He tossed back the remainder of his drink with a flick of his wrist. "We've got to find Charlie."

"So that he might offer his sage counsel and guidance, and exert himself to deal with the problem?" Edward muttered.

Gerard gave a snort. "Hardly. But it's his problem, too—he's got even more to lose than you and I do."

"When has that mattered?" But he knew his brother was right. Of course they had to tell Charlie, and since Charlie couldn't be bothered to come to Sussex, even for his father's death, it appeared they would have to go to him. And perhaps this would actually spur their brother into some action that didn't involve personal pleasure. Perhaps that was why Durham had been so desperate to beg Charlie's pardon; he knew very well how terribly his eldest son's life would change if he were to lose his name, his title, and his fortune.

Unfortunately, for all that their father seemed to think them better equipped to cope, Edward and Gerard would suffer much the same fate.

Because if they couldn't disprove this shadow on their claim to Durham, they would all lose everything.

Gerard de Lacey is a man of action, determined to save his family from ruin—and find himself a wealthy wife, just in case. Katherine Howe is a quiet widow with an independent fortune, desperate to avoid a distasteful second marriage by finding a husband of her own choosing. After an unorthodox proposal and a hasty wedding, they're off to Bath in pursuit of the blackmailer threatening Gerard's inheritance. Should love grow out of this most convenient of marriages, one can only *Blame It on Bath*.

Don't miss BLAME IT ON BATH, coming in March 2012 from Avon Books.

Caroline Linden knew from an early age she was a reader, but not a writer. Despite an addiction to Trixie Belden and Nancy Drew, she studied physics and dreamed of being an astronaut. She earned a math degree from Harvard College and then wrote software for a financial services firm, all the while reading everything in sight but especially romance. Only after she had children, and found herself with only picture books to read, did she begin to make up a story of her own. To her immense surprise, it turned out to be an entire novel—and it was much more fun than writing computer code. Now the author of seven books, she lives with her family in New England. Please visit her online at www.carolinelinden.com.